Anonymous

The Story of Cyril Rivers

And What he Learned at College

Anonymous

The Story of Cyril Rivers
And What he Learned at College

ISBN/EAN: 9783744790895

Printed in Europe, USA, Canada, Australia, Japan

Cover: Foto ©Andreas Hilbeck / pixelio.de

More available books at **www.hansebooks.com**

THE EXAMINATION.   page 6.

THE

STORY OF CYRIL RIVERS,

AND

WHAT HE LEARNED AT COLLEGE.

"LO, THIS IS THE MAN THAT MADE NOT GOD HIS STRENGTH."

PUBLISHED BY

WARREN & BLAKESLEE,

NO. 164 TREMONT STREET, BOSTON.

CONTENTS.

 CONTENTS.

THE STORY OF CYRIL RIVERS.

CHAPTER I.

A GLAD FATHER, YET A FOOLISH SON.

"The folly of fools is deceit."

CYRIL RIVERS' father is a happy man. It is Commencement week at Eaton; and he has brought his promising only son to be entered as a student in the college from which he himself graduated twenty years ago. It seems a delightful thing to him to be setting the feet of his darling in the paths that his own found so pleasant long ago. With the utmost enjoyment he has been leading the boy about, showing him the old town so soon to become familiar, engaging him a room, making arrangements for his future comfort, and in the pride of his honest heart introducing him to members of the faculty and to old friends. But now he has been forced to leave the lad in the examination-hall; so, while the paternal shadow no longer casts him into the background, so that we could only discern Cyril the quiet, well-mannered son, let us run in and take a look at Cyril the individual.

There are so many youths scattered about at the little tables, and they look so much alike with their black coats and grave faces, you may think it will be difficult to find him out. But he has enough to distinguish him in a crowd of compeers, even to eyes less partial than his father's. Tutor Watchful, who has a good memory for names and faces, can show us where he sits. This worthy man has mentally assorted those present into three sets. First — in his sympathies, at least — there are the " poor fellows," — men who have come here, some to work with one hand for the furnishing of their brains, and with the other for daily bread ; some expecting to receive help from the

faculty; some with the painful remembrance
of a widowed mother or fatherless sisters making daily sacrifices to help them gain their
education; — quiet, plain men, whom poverty
leads along a straight path, out of which she
has cleared the diversions so tempting to youth,
and in which glimpses of sunshine are only to
be reached by climbing hard hills.　Next are
those more fortunate in circumstances, if not in
nature and training, — young men bred up to
intelligence and good morals, with tastes too
refined for excess, and with enough of correct
ambition to keep them from indolence;　yet
perhaps — so the tutor sometimes fancies — too
tenderly reared, too well used to paths of life
ready smoothed for their feet, to be prepared
for genuine labor and manly self-denial.　Last,
there are the noisy fellows, riotously inclined,
who neither understand the purposes of study
nor the wisdom of obedience, nor will try to
find them out: they are, for the most part,
abundantly supplied with money, — for what
poor man could afford to send here sons of so
little promise as scholars? — and their self-

indulgent, turbulent course will be as troublesome to their teachers and as unprofitable to
themselves as they can contrive to make it.   It
chances that there are three young men, very
fair representatives of these three classes, sitting together near the end of the hall; and the
central one is Cyril Rivers.

He is a slender youth of seventeen, sits
gracefully at his desk, and is rapidly writing out
his task in translation.   His forehead is high,
and eyes bright; and though the other features
are somewhat small in proportion, they are regular and pleasing.   His face shows amiability
and intellect.   It testifies to its owner's good
ancestry; for it has no roughness where passion
could hang a scowl, and no weak outlines where
sensuality might set its seal.   His easy manner,
his correct language and pleasant voice, as he
speaks to the tutor, are evidences of gentle
breeding.   His dress is a gentleman's, neat and
suitable, but very simple.   He wears neither
stud nor scarf-pin, nor any other watch-guard
than a black ribbon.   He would have had no
watch, but that his mother, thinking he would

need it now more than she, had given him hers.
For Cyril's father is only a salaried man, a
minister in the small town of Shoreville; and
the care of his children taxes his small income
to its utmost.

It is plain that Cyril has come to the examination well prepared; for while many a face is
pale with anxiety, or red with perplexity, his
is composed and confident. He goes through
the tasks given him without any hesitation,
and is at leisure to look about him with interested eyes upon his neighbors and future
classmates. If any of them notice the easy
manner in which he is going through the examination, they call him a fortunate fellow.
Without doubt he is fortunate. If we look all
over the room we can not find another of the
one hundred there with brighter prospects.
He has strength, talent, and opportunity.
He is not rich; but what is that to one who
has grown up now, and does not care for toys?
He does not want the pretty cane that pleases
one classmate, nor the costly beaver and gor-
geous necktie that delight another. Early cul-

ture has opened his eyes to see the greater
above the lesser good. He has enough to buy
the keys of wisdom, — books and teaching, —
the means to make of his own mind a source
of treasure, — a treasure itself, a polished
diamond, many-sided, full of light, a tool that
will cut its way to any desired possession. He
stands upon a vantage ground over some of his
fellows ; for he knows what it means, — the use
he is to make of the four years that lie before
him. It elates him to grasp in anticipation the
power they will furnish him. Enlightened love
shields his life from every care while it grows,
and supplies it laboriously with every needful
enriching to develop it to a noble and fruitful
maturity. What more could a young man
ask, except the grace of God, to help him
make full use of such gifts ?

And that last and greatest need Cyril is not
ignorant of. Well might it put the crown upon
his father's joy and pride, that the boy, as he
grew up, had yielded to long and faithful instruction, and to his own clear perception of
the beautiful and good, and early enrolled him-

self among the professed disciples of the Lord. If the act had been one of the mind more than of the heart, if the lad had been so shielded from temptation by a good disposition and careful training that he had not yet begun to discover his unlikeness to the great Model he admired or the extremity of his weakness and need, — that only his heavenly Father knew. He had walked consistently in the sight of his father's church these two years: no wonder that neither of his fond parents saw reason now to fear for his principles.

I sometimes think how little those words mean — " in good and regular standing " — with which we receive and dismiss members from one church to another. We bow the head in prayer, we sit together at the communion-table, Sabbath after Sabbath, with brothers and sisters, all alike in good and regular standing to our view. But God walks among the trees in his garden ; and, though all rise tall and fair to mortal eyes, he knows which are undermined with rottenness at heart or root. With him they are not all in good and regular standing. Some day there is a sudden crash that startles the little community. A whisper of dismay runs through it. Some loud-crying sin has been discovered, some brother has fallen. There is a sorrowful wondering over him, and then his name is dropped in silence. He is in good and regular standing no more. But his downfall was not when we saw it: it was long, long before, when he suffered a little, just a little unsoundness, a little covetousness, a little vanity, a little falsehood, unrebuked, to dwell hidden in his heart.

But I have wandered from the examination. We have looked long enough at Cyril: let us glance at his neighbors. Upon his right sits a sturdy fellow, — broad-shouldered, large-headed, with hands that seem more accustomed to a plow-handle than a pen. He has hard, homely, knotty features; and they look more knotted and twisted than usual as he labors over the page of Greek before him. He is a farmer's son, from the backwoods of Maine. He is older than Cyril, being twenty-one. No one knows what induced him to take his little capital of one or two thousand dollars to invest it all, not in land or shop, but in himself. But be sure he understands what he is about, and will not fail of his returns. His preparation has been hasty and poor; but he has no time to spare, and is resolved to force his way in upon it if possible. Cyril perceives that he is hard put to it, and looks upon him with kindly concern; but his neighbor being altogether too much absorbed to perceive that, he soon turns his attention elsewhere.

Upon his left, there is another in trouble, and bearing it less wisely. It is Tom Raddon, the son of a San Francisco millionaire. Two or three years of schooling in the Eastern States have somewhat tamed the barbarism he brought from home; but he may still be recognized as the offspring of a community very different from the one in which we find him. He is tall, and has dark, heavy, and somewhat scowling features. He is as gorgeously attired as a young man can contrive to be, but he is no dandy. He has a powerful mind, but the want of early training hinders and perverts its action. He has a wonderful **moral** force **of** will and courage, **but he can not** govern **it;** and ignorant impulses, generous or selfish, drive him hither and thither at their pleasure. He is not without an aim in life: he is to be a politician, and some day to grasp and wield the power in his native State. It was his father's plan. "**I have got money,**" the **poor man** said: "he shall have station and power. **He** is **a** promising **boy; he has got a will of his** own; he stands **six** feet three inches high; he has got a thundering **voice and a fierce temper.** I will send him to the East **to be** educated. **He** shall learn to make speeches, **to** quote Latin and precedents and the Constitution, **to** talk about Solon and Socrates and such names; and then **let** him come home, and begin to practice **law here, and** make himself heard. I have got money to back him for any office, cost what it may. **He's** sure to succeed. I shall see him in Congress **some** day, and perhaps in the White House. He stands as good a chance to be president as anybody."

Nevertheless, the examination deals severely

with this future ruler; and Cyril sees him scowl
and hears him mutter oaths over his work.
We can not blame him for them as we might
another, for they were among the first words
he learned to speak. Cyril is sorry, and his
good taste is offended; but he is not shocked,
for such expressions of vexation are so very
frequent in school and at play that he has become sadly accustomed to them. At last, however, Tom looks up, and meets his friendly gaze,
and sees his finished paper. Then there is
some kind of swift communication between the
two. Cyril casts a furtive glance round the
room at the busy examiners, and in a minute
has transferred Tom's paper to his desk.
There is a whispered explanation of this line,
and that, and the other; and the rough face
grows smooth, and Tom can not refrain a little
growl of relief and satisfaction as he takes
back his paper and proceeds with his work.
As the day wears on, there is occasion to repeat
these maneuvers a great many times, more or
less flagrantly. Sometimes a whispered word
is all; sometimes there is a whole problem

worked out on Cyril's **desk, and** transferred to **his** neighbor's. **The** reality **of what** he was doing seemed not to occur to Cyril: he **had** given such help, and seen it given, so many times from boyhood up, the general opinion among his associates never blaming, often upholding **the deed as** amiable and kind. **He could not tell how small he** was when his **mother had taught** him **the** terrible words about "whosoever **maketh a lie;"** but he did not stop **to** consider **whether he could be** charged with such a sin in this **easy, good-**natured little action. **Yet** what else **but** "making lies" was he doing in putting his knowledge upon Tom's papers? One by one they went into the professor's hands, bearing their false testimony. They differed from **the** falsehoods we are quickest **to** condemn, as hav-**ing no** malicious motive; **but** they were just as baneful in their nature, inflicting both upon the fabricator and the adopter an injury whose tangling threads of consequence ran far on into the future, and filled it with snares and traps of stumbling.

The day, so trying to many, wears away at
last. Toward six o'clock all sit in suspense,
waiting for the distribution of the blue and
white papers which make known its results.
There are many who were sanguine this morn-
ning who are very downcast now, and many
who have been patient and composed who are
becoming nervous. Cyril suffers no anxiety,
but he is tired, and desirous to get away. Tom
Raddon is very restless, bites his nails, and
fidgets in his chair, and mutters his weariness
and suspense to his neighbor. The Maine man
is as resolute-looking as ever, though a shade
paler than this morning: if he has good reason
for discouragement, he will not show it in his
face. And now the grave tutor comes toward
these three, dealing joy with his white papers
and regret with the blue. There is one of the
latter for John Seelye, the Maine man ; and it
is sadly freighted with conditions, having,
moreover, written upon it the advice from
the faculty that he had better not attempt the
examination again without another year's preparation. His case looks very desperate, but

his mind is made up not to take that advice. He means to have another trial at the end of the two months' vacation.

Both for Cyril and Tom, there are certificates of their having passed the examination satisfactorily. Tom is so overcome with delight at his good fortune, that he almost jumps out of his seat with joy, and can hardly suppress the profane exclamation of astonishment that rises to his lips.

And now the crowd begins to disperse. There are mutual congratulations among the fortunate ones, and words of friendly encouragement for those who have been less successful. Cyril lingers a moment by the table where John Seelye still sits, somehow interested in him, and curious to know the result of his day's experiences. He makes some little remark to him, and is answered pleasantly; but John evidently is not inclined to enter into conversation, and says he is waiting to speak to the professors, so Cyril passes on. Tom Raddon keeps close beside, and, when they are fairly outside the door, seizes his hand, and shakes it heartily.

"I'm your friend for life!" he cries, sublimely certain that the announcement must be glorious news for Cyril. "I'd no idea of getting in without four or five conditions! It's the bulliest news to send to my father! it's as good as an extra hundred dollars a year for me; and it's all your doing!"

Cyril modestly disclaimed so much credit. He was pleased with the show of gratitude, but would willingly have withdrawn his hand from the strong grasp that held it. He dearly liked to win golden opinions from all sorts of men; but this was not exactly the fellow he wanted claiming ardent friendship with him just now. He saw men more of his own kind near at hand; and he wanted a chance to make acquaintance with some of them before they scattered, not to meet till the term began. But Tom held him tight, and went on talking loud and fast, expatiating upon his past history and future prospects, his scrapes at school, and his fears in college. Then there were mischievous sophomores loitering about to watch the new men coming forth from the hall, and

to mock at them with jeering songs and
speeches. These incensed Tom, and Cyril was
obliged to use his best logic to prevent him
from challenging a fight. So at last they
passed out of the grounds together; and, when
Cyril went home with his father, the only acquaintance he had made among his future
classmates was Tom Raddon.

CHAPTER II.

THE TRUE AND THE DECEITFUL WITNESS.

"A true witness delivereth souls; but a deceitful witness speaketh lies."

"He winketh with his eyes, he speaketh with his feet, he teacheth with his fingers."

IT was the hour for the freshmen's first regular recitation. With anxious punctuality, most of Cyril's division were already gathered near the door of their recitation-room, talking in low tones, making acquaintance with each other. Some a little apart, with open books, were at the last minute still studying. Among these was John Seelye, who had got into college by the force of such terribly hard work during the last eight weeks as few could have endured. And now he will be obliged to work just as hard to maintain his position. Cyril was glad to see him again. Although he knew so little of him, he felt a curious respect and sympathy for him. He had an instinct that this was a man whose liking and approbation were worth having. He had never found it a mistake to express any kindly feeling that came into his heart; and he meditated getting near John when they should pass in at the door, and expressing his pleasure at seeing him there. But, while he was thinking of this, a heavy hand was laid upon his shoulder; and, looking up, he saw his other examination acquaintance, Tom Raddon.

"Halloo, old fellow!" he cried, heartily shaking Cyril's hand. "How are you. Glad to see you!"

"Thank you," said Cyril pleasantly. "I've been looking round to see if I should find you here." He did not say, however, that he had experienced a little feeling of relief at not finding him. "It begins to look jolly here," he added, "now that all the fellows have got together."

"Yes," said Tom; but then looked down at the Legendre in his hand, and seemed a little doubtful. "If it wasn't for these things, you know," he continued. "But I suppose you're all right there: you found it as easy as fun. Well, I hope I'm posted too, this once: I'd like to make a fair start the first day. If they'd only let me have the figure! They say they'll only give a fellow the number of the proposition here to start upon. Old Easiegoe, where I prepared, always used to let us have the figure. I don't know how I shall remember any thing without it. I say," — as the tutor made his appearance, and the crowd moved after him into the recitation-room, — "if you see me running aground, just give me a shove."

The·recitation was likely to go pretty smoothly that day, of course. Almost all, like Tom, were anxious to run well at the beginning of the race. There was probably many a freshman, with the unusual consciousness of knowing his lesson, who would have been quite disappointed at not being called upon to recite. But the tutor, understanding the state of the case, seemed to light by instinct upon those least likely to be fluent. Among the first called up was John Seelye. He rose and gave

the proposition correctly, though slowly, and as
if to bring out each word in its order required
a separate effort of memory. Then, as he went
forward to the blackboard to demonstrate, the
fellows near heard him take a long breath, as
if about to set himself to a very hard task.
He took the chalk and began well, proceeding
through the first half of the proof without any
trouble. Then came a part of the demonstra-
tion beginning from a new point; and his memory could not at once recall the connecting link
that bound it to what had gone before. He
paused, looking disturbed, and knitting his brow
in the effort of thought to recall the lost idea.
Whether he would have been successful we
can not tell, for at that minute a good-natured
little fellow, who sat close by the blackboard,
whispered the words that held the hint John's
mind was in search of. He supposed, however,
that John did not hear them, from his behavior. He laid down the chalk, and turned
directly away from the board. " I can not do
it," he said to the teacher, and returned to his
seat. His face looked somewhat dark and

severe ; for there was great regret, not unmingled with anger, in his heart. His footing in college was so precarious, every failure weighed against his being allowed to remain. He was sure, that, if he had been left to himself, he should not have failed ; but, as it was, no other alternative had been left him. He could not proceed without making **use of** another man's knowledge **as** his own ; and both pride and principle were too strong in his mind to let him **do** that. No unlucky accident **should force him** into deceit, even for all **the benefits of the** whole college **course.** So what was offered **as** a kindness **proved a** misfortune to him : **but he bore it in silence ;** and no **one in the** class-room **knew how much** vexation **he was** trying to subdue. **Cyril** was sorry to see him fail, and **so was the** teacher. The young man who had prompted him muttered, " Stupid of him not **to hear ! "** The proposition was given **to** another, **who** finished it **fluently.**

Meanwhile **Tom Raddon had been** attracted **by a** beautiful chronometer that **one** of his neighbors had pulled out, and was intent upon examining it, asking questions **about** it of **its** owner **in not** very subdued whispers. **To** that he probably owed it that he was the next man called up. So much engaged was he, that he was startled when aroused to the consciousness that his name had been spoken, and rose to his feet in some confusion. " Proposition twenty-ninth," **demands the tutor.** Tom can not collect his **wits.** **He thinks** he knew which **one** that **was a minute ago, but now it** has slipped from his mind. **He looks** imploringly **down** at Cyril, who, as the fates would have **it, because** their names follow **in** alphabetical order, **is to be** his seatmate in class and in chapel for **the** next four years. Cyril is apparently quite unconscious of Tom's perplexity. His eyes are bent upon the white wristband which has pushed itself down below his sleeve, and **upon** which he is making a few swift **lines with** his pencil. Now he changes his position, and **throws** the hand with the exposed cuff carelessly down upon his knee. In the midst **of** Tom's bewilderment his eyes fall upon it. Lo, there is the figure **of** proposition twenty-ninth !

He catches the clew at once, and his presence of mind is restored with his memory. He begins and ends his recitation with perfect success, and takes his seat with the triumphant certainty that he has, as he expresses it, " made a rush." The underhand help he has received does not seem to take any thing from his satisfaction with himself: on the contrary, he is delighted with his quickness in accepting it, and with Cyril's adroitness in offering it.

Well, there is again excuse to be made for Tom. Who could expect him to abhor such a little cheat, when from his very childhood he had heard his father boast more over dishonest profits than any other, and seen him chuckle over the advantages he gained from the ignorance of poor John. Chinaman, giving him drink in order to draw him into unjust and cruel contracts; but for that Cyril's guilt seems the greater. There was no such palliation for his conduct: the example set before him had been shining white, the teaching faithful and grave. Yet he, who knew the light, deliberately put out his hand, and pushed his brother farther on into the darkness. I wonder that diagram, as he sketched it, did not illustrate for him a moral instead of a mathematical truth, and that he did not substitute words of a new meaning for those Tom was reciting so fluently. Why did they not run in his mind something in this wise ? —

Two sins whose motives are parallel, and tending in the same direction, are equal to each other.

Let A B, the desire of favor, and B C, the wish to seem adroit and knowing, unite to form

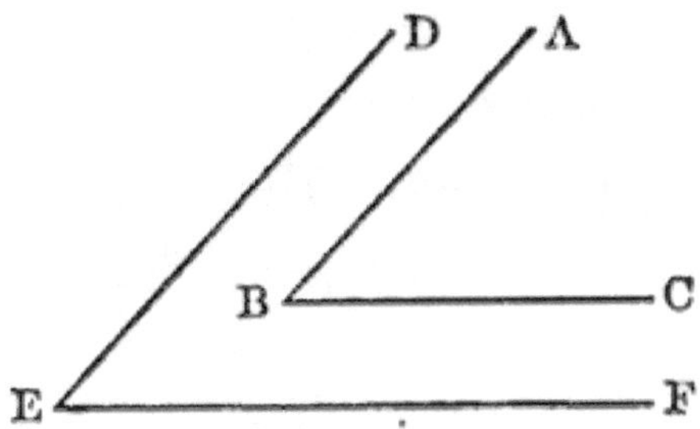

my sin ; and let D E, the love of money, and E F, the wish to seem generous, unite to form Ananias'. Then, since A B is parallel to D E, and B C to E F, and the sins they result in alike tend to deception, those sins are equal, and their capacity for sorrowful consequences as great.

Perhaps you will call that a very strained and fanciful statement; but nevertheless it seems to me the fact is as true as any in Euclid.

· But Cyril had never trained himself to apply great principles to small affairs; and evil example and the desire to be popular helped him to overlook what was wrong in such habits as these. He did feel a little uncomfortable about what he had just done; but that was not so much because of its sinfulness as on account of the fact that he had put another bond between Tom and himself, when he had not quite made up his mind that he wanted to continue the intimacy. But he comforted himself with thinking that one could not have too many friends, and that he could no doubt shake off this one easily enough when he became troublesome.

The recitation-hour passed away, and the tutor's word of dismissal set the class dispersing. Cyril was again looking toward John Seelye; but Tom had already got his powerful arm about his friend's shoulder, and was pulling him toward the staircase. Tom was eager to pour out his exultation over his own and Cyril's cleverness, and **Cyril must** perforce pass **on** and hear it. But, before we go with them, let us stop a minute, and listen to what John Steelye is saying to the youth who sat beside the black-board when John was trying to recite. At the dismissal of the class he went across the room, and took **the lad by** the button-hole. There **was great earnestness in** John's face, but not a trace of vexation **now.** He might have come to express his thanks for **a kindly** intention, for all that his **countenance showed to the** contrary. But he said, looking down from **the** height **of** his six feet and his twenty-one years upon the youngster of seventeen, " I want to tell you something, my lad. Don't you ever again, as long as you live, offer to help me, or any other man, with a present of a lie."

Nollie Stavins looked **at him** in utter astonishment. He could not **at** first comprehend his meaning.

" Oh ! " he said at last, recovering from his surprise. " Why, I just gave you **a** hint ! I thought you'd be glad of it."

"Yes, I know; but I tell you I can't be glad to make show of another man's goods for my own, whether it's his knowledge or any thing else. You meant it kindly: I thank you for that. But the next time you've got a good feeling toward anybody, don't you let the devil get hold of it for an instrument to help make a cheat of you and your friends. You're a traitor to it if you do, and go against the very ends for which God gave it to you."

Stavins began to look serious, though not displeased. "Ain't you too strict?" he asked.

"No, I am not," said John with decision. "I love the truth always. I believe the man that won't stick to it in every little thing, before you know it his whole character will be unsound. If you'll remember that, you won't do again what you did for me to-day, nor you won't be angry with me for speaking about it."

"I am not angry," said Stavins, who was an earnest and well-meaning little fellow. "I believe you're right, and I'm glad you spoke."

Ah, if Cyril had only heard these words of John, or rather if he had had such a spirit!

If he, with such earnestness and uprightness, had spoken like things to **Tom Raddon, what a happy thing it might have been for** them both! But, if we follow them as they pass out, we find Cyril thoughtlessly laying more snares, instead of making straight the path for his own and his companion's feet. A number of **the** young men had joined them, some attracted by Cyril's bright face, and some by Tom's tall figure and dashing dress, and the boisterous spirits in which **he was** indulging. "**Hold my** hat," he cried, "while I stand **on my head, in** honor of that bully rush!"

Some one caught the hat, and down went **Tom's** great head, with all its black, shaggy locks, into the green grass, while his long legs slowly elevated themselves in **air.** A shout of laughter broke forth at **the absurdity of the** maneuver. "**There,**" said Tom, picking himself up; "I'll do that for you again whenever you say, Rivers! Did you see the cute way he helped me out of a scrape, boys?"

"No: how was that?" asked **the** others, greatly amused.

Tom seized Cyril's unwilling arm, pushed up the coat-sleeve, and showed the diagram marked upon the white cuff, explaining volubly how much at a loss he had been, and how it had helped him. They all listened with laughing interest: there was not one who seemed to consider the matter in any way a serious one.

"It was cleverly done," said one. "I shall be on the look-out for your wristbands, too, Rivers."

"I should say," said another shrewdly, "that was a trick which would serve one's self as well as other people, eh, Rivers?"

"I suppose it might," said Cyril, smiling; "but I never tried using it in that way. It's one I keep expressly to lend. It's not so good as the one I keep for myself, which is to learn my lessons; but I can tell you another I used to see at school that beats the wristband dodge, if you want one for your own benefit."

"What is that? tell us that!" cried Tom.

"Who's got shiny boots?" said Cyril, looking down at the various pairs of feet clustered near him. Tom put forward one of his, and showed a gigantic boot highly varnished.

"Just the thing!" said Cyril, laughing. "Rest it up there on the fence, will you?"

Tom obediently mounted it to the top rail, quite regardless of jokes and laughter at the expense of its size, some one calling it a "guffin," and another bidding him take it down just a moment so that he could get a view of the chapel-clock.

"It's an understanding of the first order," said Tom good-naturedly.

"Yes," said Cyril; "and I'll show you how to make it serve you better than the one you keep in the upper story. See here, now!" and, producing a soft lead-pencil, he began tracing diagrams upon the surface of the boot. Then, turning it so that the light would strike upon it, the dark lines were plainly visible.

"It's as plain as the book!" cried Tom, delighted; "and no more chance of Agin's seeing it than of his seeing what's inside your head!"

You see," said Cyril: "you just take your

foot up in your lap, and appear to be examining the make or the wear of your shoe, and you can be studying your lesson all class-time. And when you stand up to recite, if you should be looking thoughtfully down upon the floor, why, there wouldn't be any thing very suspicious in that, you know."

"I vow, I'll try it to-morrow!" cried Tom.

"And so will I!" said another.

Cyril looked up, still lightly smiling, and yet a little disturbed. "No," said he, putting up his pencil: "I guess I wouldn't. I only just showed you for fun. It used to make sport among the boys trying it in the grammar school at home. But I tell you it's a better trick, and considerably less trouble in the long run, to learn one's lessons: there's no danger of its ever falling through, you see."

"Yes: that's all very well for you to say," said Raddon; "but I ain't smart enough to learn that trick, so it's well you've got others to teach me. I don't believe I should have got here if it hadn't been for you; so don't you think, now, the responsibility of keeping me here kind o' rests on you?"

"Nonsense! I hope not!" cried Cyril hastily. "Come, don't let's stand loitering here; come on and pass ball."

He pulled a base-ball from his pocket, and they went to another part of the grounds to play. Cyril threw himself into the exercise, and soon forgot the mischief he had been scattering.

But it was not lost so quickly as it slipped out of his memory. Two days after this, Tom insisted on taking Cyril up to his room to show him something. There Cyril found a huge pair of boots upon the table; and Tom, taking them to the window, showed how neatly he had copied out upon them all the diagrams of his lesson.

"There!" said he triumphantly, "now I'm prepared to make a rush. I can go down and play billiards with an easy mind."

Cyril stood looking at the boots with a half-smile upon his face, but with a very uncomfortable feeling in his heart nevertheless. "You've forgotten something, Raddon," he said carelessly.

"What's that?" said Tom. "I thought I'd got them all there."

"Yes; but what good will they do you without the numbers? You have not numbered them."

"Thunder! what a fool I am!" exclaimed Tom. "I'm too stupid to do my own cheating without the help of your wit. Where's that book?"

By this time the unpleasant feeling was growing stronger in Cyril's mind, and he did not assist in the search for the book among the mass of things upon the table.

"Look here, Tom," he said: "never mind the book. I wouldn't get the numbers: let it go. You can learn to do without the figures as well as any of us; and, if you get used to going on by such ways as these, it'll be awful rough for you at examination."

Ah, Cyril! with all the teaching you have had, can you do nothing better than to urge motives of policy so feebly? If you had but a tithe of John Seelye's love of the plain principles of right, and the least spark of his boldness in proclaiming them, who knows how they might lay hold upon Tom's untaught heart! But he will not heed your timid whisper of prudence and caution.

He looked at Cyril in surprise, and then scowled and grew sulky. "What! have all that trouble for nothing? No: I won't. It's well enough for you to say you would, and you wouldn't: you don't need to. But I tell you I *can't* learn to do without the figures: I might study myself blind, and I should never be sure of my lesson. And as for the examination, it may go hang!"

And so saying, Tom angrily pitched the heap of books upon the table right and left, brought forth the Euclid, and slammed it down with a bang, by way of letting off his irritation. Cyril stood still a minute, and watched him turning the leaves. He said to himself that he had now, at all events, done his duty in remonstrating with Tom, but that there could be no use in trying to do any thing with a fellow of that description : one must just let him go his own way. He staid a few minutes, till, by a little pleasant talk, he had won him out of his fit of ill-humor, and then went away.

CHAPTER III.

THE POPULAR MAN.

“The blackslider in heart shall be filled with his own ways; and
a good man shall be satisfied from himself.”

 DAY or two after the events re-
corded in the last chapter, Tom
came and seated himself in Cyril’s
room, evidently with some plan in his
mind which he wanted to unfold.

“ Rivers,” said he, “ what are you going to
do about the initiation ? ”   He meant the so-
called initiatory exercises, through which the
sophomores, some night this week, were going
to put the new-comers, tossing them in a blanket, and playing upon them their practical jokes,
or forcing them, if they preferred, to “ stand a
treat.”

“ Why, take it as it comes, I suppose,” said
Cyril smiling. “ I’m not afraid of a blanket,

if it's a strong one, nor of sham coffins and sepulchers, either."

"Nor *I*," said Tom; "but then I rather think it's a more satisfactory thing to all concerned if a fellow chooses to treat. I'd about as lief be sitting down to a comfortable supper of woodcock and hot oysters, making the fellows happy, if they are sophs, as to be pitched round the streets blindfold, very likely getting mad, and stirring 'em up to haze me real rough."

"Very wise of you too," said Cyril. "I'd advise you to treat, by all means." He knew, as no doubt Tom did, that the latter was a marked man with the sophomores, both on account of his noisy, boastful manners, and the enormous wealth it was said he had at command. It had been resolved that he should treat very generously, or be roughly handled.

"Then," said Tom, "will you go with me, and make a joint thing of it?"

"Why, no," said Cyril, much surprised and somewhat discomposed at such a proposition. "I can't afford to treat."

"Confound it!" said Tom, "you know I don't mean that. I just want you to come along with me, and have it our treat, — a joint thing. You know how to do such a thing, and I don't. You know how to make it a gentlemanly affair; but, if it's only me, they'll act like Injuns over a war-feast. If I've got the 'rocks,' can't you lend me your brains? I can't manage it by myself: I shouldn't get decent treatment for all my pains, and there'd be some kind of a row out of it. Why can't you come with me?"

"Because I can't," said Cyril slowly. But, made in this way, the offer did not seem so impossible to accept, and it was not without its temptations. It would have been nothing to him, but lately, to have had it known among the fellows that he was too poor to soften his initiation with a treat, and help establish good feeling between his class and the next higher; and, as we have seen, he had just acknowledged it to Tom. But he had not done so without a twinge of annoyance: his ideas were lowering, with his aims, since he left his father's influence. Cyril's uncertainty about desiring to be named among Tom's intimates had also vanished. He had not lived more than seventeen years in the sordid atmosphere of this world, without perceiving that there was something magical in the name of a millionaire. He saw that Tom, by virtue of his wealth, and also of his high spirits and native strength of character, was going to take a better social standing in the class than Cyril had at first thought possible. In the little college world, he was going to be a man of some consideration. It would, at least, be nothing to be ashamed of to be ranked among his companions. Then what Tom had said of the necessity of his help both flattered and tempted Cyril. Here was an opportunity of shining. Cyril was conscious of social talents, of a ready wit, and a sort of enthusiasm in sport that always pleased. Moreover, it was true that he had a gift at managing such sport, and could keep order, as Tom said, where the latter's displeasure and growling would be apt to turn the whole affair into a wild riot. But, then, how could he let Tom pay for what was called their joint treat?   He was conscious that would be unwise, if not disgraceful.

"If you won't join," said Tom, scowling, "I wont have any treat.   I'll stand the hazing."

Cyril looked at his dogged, frowning face, and was troubled.   "They'll be rough on you, Tom," he said: "it won't do at all.   They know you're rich; and it's said round among the fellows that they expect a first-rate treat of you."

"Confound 'em! I don't care.   If you do, you might just come with me.   I know one thing: if they're rough on me, I'll show 'em *that*, in a way they won't like;" and Tom pulled from his pocket a small revolver, with shining silver ornaments and polished wood.

"But that is not fair!" said Cyril, surprised and alarmed.   "I say, Raddon,"—reaching out for it anxiously,—"give me that to keep till the initiation is over!"

"No: I won't; and, what's more, I vow I'll have it in my pocket that night, unless you'll promise to come to my treat."

Cyril was perplexed and half angry. Tom's willful hanging upon him and teasing him in this way was, however, only the result he might have expected from his unkind kindness to him the day they first met, and since.

"Come," said Tom, perceiving his irresolution, "be friendly, and do a fellow a favor, can't you?"

"To keep you from hanging yourself!" said Cyril, vexed, and yet laughing.

But Tom saw that he had carried the day.

"Exactly," said he. "And, now it's all settled, come down and play billiards with us."

"No," said Cyril: "I brought some books from the library two days ago that I have hardly looked into."

"Oh!" groaned Tom, between a sigh and a yawn: "books! I'm told I came here to read books as well as study 'em. I went over to the library, and asked the 'seed' there to give me something to enlighten me about the politics of this country; and he told me I'd best read somebody on common law, and somebody on the Constitution, and somebody's

Thirty Years in the United-States' Senate, and more besides. I said I'd take **all** he mentioned : how should I know some **of** 'em were so big? Gracious! I thought I'd never get 'em lugged up to my room. I'm bound to do something to be the man my father expects; **but** hang me if **I can go** through all those, besides the Greek and Euclid!"

Cyril was amused, but he kept a sober face. "It's good reading," said he. "I shouldn't wonder **if you liked it if you'd** once set to work at **it.** Better not go **down to** play billiards, but **just try the 'Thirty Years'** instead."

"Better not!" **Is** that all, Cyril? Can **you** not tell him **why** he'd better not? Tell **him** here are four long evening hours given **to him by God;** that he has had recreation enough **to-day;** that he bowled after dinner when he should **have studied** his Euclid, and played bazique in his **room this** morning when he should have been **writing his** Latin prose, and **lounged away** many precious minutes between the occupations of the day. Tell him that if he wastes now these last hours, so full of opportunity, before the nightfall comes to end the chance to work, that if in them he wears away in frivolous excitement any more of the strength of the good mind God gave him, — dims in them the likeness it was made to bear, — his Father and Creator will hold him fearfully responsible for the sin ; tell him how he will himself one day grieve over the irretrievable loss. You are not ignorant, Cyril. Why will you not bethink yourself, and tell him ?

But Cyril has no other word of warning than his careless " better not ; " and Tom pays no heed to that. He says there is going to be a game for the championship in his club, between the two best players, and that he must be there to see ; and so he goes away.

The intimacy between these two, so unlike in character, tastes, and breeding, grew fast in the following days. Tom not only depended much on Cyril, but he showed for him a sincere admiration and affection that pleased and flattered him, and was not without its effect in causing a return of love. Yet by Cyril's help Tom stood in a false position : he had got into college only half-prepared. Therefore he justly felt that Cyril bore a sort of responsibility for him. It would not have mattered much, perhaps, if he had been at all industrious, — if he even did as well as he had resolved to do. But he could not govern himself. Indolence and the love of pleasure were too strong for him. There were companions to solicit him to sports of every kind, some of them very near to vice, and poverty imposed on him no salutary check. So the struggle to get a little farther toward his aim, yet to live without the least self-denial, was every day being fought over with him. When he was threatened with too disgraceful defeat, then he ran to Cyril for assistance. Cyril sometimes tried to help him in a lawful way, but oftener, being himself full of occupations, gave him his own Latin prose exercises and demonstrated problems to copy, without any apparent compunctions.

Whatever reluctance might have lingered in Cyril's mind to join Tom in his treat vanished in the excitement of the hour when initiation night came on. Tom, to make sure of his plan, was in Cyril's room when the masked sophomores invaded it in search of the " freshmen." What representations he made to them Cyril cared little, at that moment, in the anticipation of sport. The two were blindfolded and marched down the street together, lectured all the way with mock counsels and absurd admonitions, and obliged to answer impertinent inquiries into the state of the freshman's purse and wardrobe, and into his circumstances and condition generally. Cyril was just in the mood to make happy replies, full of good-nature, yet keen and fearless; so that Tom's disposition to grow foolishly sulky at being treated like a juvenile was laughed away; and the mirth of the whole party lost any element there might have been in it of malicious teasing, and became genial and friendly. Tom and Cyril being taken into some restaurant, as they perceived by the heat and smell, were seated at a table, and commanded to make a speech of welcome to their self-bidden guests, and to

order them refreshments.   This latter duty
Tom performed with reckless liberality, ordering the choicest viands the house could supply;
while Cyril, quite as ready for his part, climbed
upon a chair and began a speech.   He knew
how to suit the taste of his audience: he had
entered heartily into the mirthful spirit of the
occasion, and he had a ready wit and fluent
tongue.   He expressed his brotherly welcome
and his pompous offer of hospitality in an absurd jargon of stilted and poetic phrases, min-
gled with Greek and Latin quotations, and set
off with the choicest college slang.   It was
full of happy allusions to college jokes and cus-
toms and characters, and occasionally, under
high-flown compliments to the auditors, covered
some sly hit upon them which was too good
not to be pardoned.   There were many other
parties of young men in the room, all of whom
were attracted to listen; and, when Cyril came
down from his chair, he was applauded with
cries of " Well done, Freshie! well done ! "
" Bully for the Fresh ! "   Tom and he, having
first been obliged to drink the health of the

sophomore class, were then allowed to take off their blinders, and condescendingly invited to eat, drink, and make themselves at home. And, as the feast proceeded, not all the sham dignity of the little party could disguise the fact that they found Cyril the freshman very good company. Toward the close of the evening, he mounted the chair again, and, not having the blinder this time to hide his bright eyes and facile countenance, began describing the various members of the faculty, in the act of expressing their strictures upon such demonstrations as were setting the college in an uproar to-night; mimicking the anxious sigh of one, the patient gravity of another, the sharp indignation of a third, and giving little oddities of manner and figure, little tricks of speech and tone, with so much faithfulness that the delighted young men could call out the name of each one personified, as the actor made him appear in his turn upon the stage.

. This put the climax to his glory and popularity for the evening. Nothing could exceed Tom's delight at the performance ; and the report of it gained Cyril great renown among his classmates. He became, from that evening, one of the most conspicuous and admired among them. But it was no good fortune. So long as he had been comparatively unknown, there had been no great temptation to lead him to deviate from the regular habits of reading and study which his own taste and ambition had led him to establish. But now his room began to be sought out by all manner of visitors, — some the gayest and idlest, some the best and most attractive men in the class. Everybody wanted his acquaintance and company. He was beset with solicitations for his leisure time. Would he not join this society, or that? Would he not be a member of the singing-club, or the chess-club, or the billiard-club, or the boating-club? Would he not go to walk, or to ride, or to be introduced to lady friends in the city? Every kind of pleasure that lively or intelligent or wealthy companionship could offer was at his command. And Cyril was young: if he liked books, nevertheless life looked to him a thousand times more charming. How, then, was it likely to fare with one who, in spite of good teaching, in spite of many noble aspirations, in spite of a clear insight of consequences, yet had not trained himself to bring conscience to bear in little things? who, now that no watchful father had oversight of his hours, could say, "It is no harm to slight, just this once, the perfect mastery I know I might get over this lesson; no harm, just this once, to let my companions keep me up so late that I shall hardly wake in time for prayers to-morrow; no harm, just for to-day, to lose the reading I was going to keep up with my study, and which would make it so much more valuable"? Why, the harm which he denied overtook him, — great harm and irrecoverable loss. For the yielding to small temptation never happens "just this once," but again, and again, and again. And each time it wears away some strength, some soundness and goodness, from the foundations of character, and renders them at last weak and untrustworthy.

Cyril became the most popular man in his

class. He wrote its songs, furnished it with squibs, and planned its prowess. He was the glory of its base-ball nine, the best debater and the most active politician in its literary society. But, little by little, he was ceasing to be its best scholar. He had so much to occupy his time, there were so many to please, so many enjoyments to be tasted, such various kinds of glory to win. He could not degenerate into one of those scrambling students, who run to recitation with open book; who tremble for fear they shall be called up; who call it wonderfully good luck if they blunder forth some confused notion of the lesson, and just their luck if they are compelled to sit down in ignominious failure; who cast glances at their classmates for underhand help; bring papers of hints in their handkerchiefs, and formulas in their hats; yet never, with all their devices, get any thing but the credit, or rather the discredit, they deserve. Cyril's ambition was still too strong to do that. It troubled him from time to time to discover how he was slighting the purpose for which he was sent to college. He did not like to give up all that it meant to be a good scholar, even for the sweetness of being called a good companion.

But there was a better thing — the surety of every attainment worth making — that he was giving up, not consciously perhaps, but thoughtlessly. It was the fear of the Lord. Perhaps Cyril had never, in truth, followed hard after God, — set him upon his right hand continually, so that he could not be moved. Only while he had lived with those who walked close to their Master, and displayed his light and beauty, he, too, had seemed to be in nearness and covenant, as his kindred were. But now, when others showed no devotion but to pleasure and selfish gain, Cyril was like them, almost in every thought. True, there was a Bible among his books, and he maintained a decorous regard for the Sabbath, and gave a respectful assent to all religious opinions advanced by chance in his presence; and all his companions knew that Cyril was one of the small — too small — number of communicants among them. But where were the outspoken horror of sin, the watchfulness, the humility, that should be found in the heart and life of one in whose love the Lord was really first? Above all, where was the service, the eager, involuntary work, performed, hourly, whenever opportunity offered, the vote and influence always for the right, the word of enlightenment or earnest warning or entreaty spoken out of fullness of heart? Ah! what allurement could there have been to Cyril in the idea of being the most popular man in his class, compared with that of being the most useful, if there had been still before his eyes the beauty he had once discerned in forgetting self, and living for God and his fellow-men? That vision had no power now: it had not come out of gratitude to Christ, who had given him salvation, for Cyril had never yet really felt his need of that salvation.

While Cyril suffered mortification and discomfiture to find himself losing in scholarship, and while a vague uneasiness and anxiety, the unheeded reproaches of conscience, disturbed him in his few unoccupied and solitary hours,

John Seelye was day by day tasting the proudest and sweetest pleasure he had ever known, finding himself, in his studies, rapidly gaining ground. He had suffered, at first, every discouragement, and worked with such self-denial, such labor and patience, as his more fortunate classmates could hardly have imagined. But now his way was brightening with hope: the path grew more smooth and easy, and the prospect of the reward was becoming more certain.

John was hardly ever seen except at recitation, from which he came and went with a preoccupied and silent manner. Therefore very few in the class knew much about him. Nollie Stavins, however, had found out his room, and formed a friendship with him, and was sometimes laughed at for often quoting and praising him, and for showing vexation if any one by chance spoke contemptuously of his slow recitations or his shabby coat and plain face. But, though John was so little known, most of those who met him every day liked and respected him. Little acts and occasional words showed him to possess a kindly and an honest heart, as well as an independent spirit. Perhaps his face would have been missed from the classroom with as much regret as any of the brighter and handsomer ones that were accustomed to be met there. Between Cyril and John, there was a quiet understanding of mutual kindly feeling; but John was too hard at work, and Cyril too much occupied with the pressure of new engagements, to extend the acquaintance beyond a friendly nod or salutation as they met each other at their daily tasks.

CHAPTER IV.

THE UNWILLING BOATMAN.

" Happy is he that condemneth not himself in that thing which he alloweth."

HE first winter of Cyril's college life passed away. If it had offered temptations to slight duty for pleasure, the opening spring presented them in double strength. The country about made itself beautiful, and attracted to walks and drives; and the soft moonlight nights tempted to late loitering and talking and singing under the elms. But most irresistibly the sparkling waters of the broad river, flowing between green hills and meadows, drew the young men to the sports it afforded. The summer races were approaching; and in every class there was excitement about the selection and training of the competing crews, and the con-

dition of the racing-boats. The freshmen were
not the less interested and ambitious in looking
forward to the contest because it was a new
thing to them. They were zealous to show
themselves possessed of as much vigor and
enterprise, as well as of as much unity of feeling and liberality, as any of the other classes.
Their efforts were not to be considered juvenile: they meant to win success and glory if
determination could do it.

Such, at least, appeared to be the spirit
shown at an informal meeting of those interested, held one night in Tom Raddon's room
to discuss ways and means of providing a new
boat, and to decide upon the names of those
who seemed best qualified to compose the crew.
Four out of those who had shown capacity to
become good oarsmen were easily chosen.
They were, first, Minor, nicknamed the " Major," a thin, gray-eyed, close-mouthed fellow,
with such a stock of quiet willfulness that it
was thought his only looking at a thing would
make it work according to his mind; then
Baum, a large, rather dull-looking man, whose

strength was all physical, and lay in his tremendous arms and shoulders; Benson, a stout, merry lad, whose muscle and energy were not worth more than his hopeful, cheerful temper; and Sine, a fine-looking fellow, except for a certain indifference and languor in his handsome face, which was sadly accounted for when he hesitated to enroll himself among the crew because he should then be obliged to give up smoking. But about the choice of the two remaining oarsmen, there was a great deal of doubt and discussion. One name after another was proposed and refused. Some of his flatterers offered Tom's; but, to the great relief of the rest, he promptly declined. He liked yachting well enough, he said; but he was too big and blundering for a shell-boat. At last, some one said, " Where's Rivers? Why would not he be the right man ? "

" Just the one ! " said Benson: " where is he ? "

Cyril had kept away purposely. He did not want to go upon the crew. He had not the necessary time to spare ; and then boating was an expensive sport, and he shrank from being constantly drawn into such, when his means would not allow him to bear any portion of the costs. He knew the pleasure his companions had in his society gladly excused that; yet he did not want it to happen any oftener than he could help.

But he had been brought up by the seashore, and loved boats. He was agile and strong, and had the gift of inspiring enthusiasm. He would make a valuable member of the crew, his companions thought. They must have him at any rate. He would make boating popular with half of the class if he would engage in it heartily. Some one must run and tell him he was wanted in Raddon's room.

While the messenger was gone, they were debating whom to choose next, when Nollie Stavins astonished them by proposing John Seelye. Nollie was a man of some consideration in the boating world, because he owned a beautiful new "double-scull:" therefore his suggestion was not scoffed at, as it would otherwise have been.

"Seelye!" said one: "why, what sort of a man would he be?"

"A first-rate man!" said Nollie. "He's as strong as a horse, and as cool-headed a fellow as I ever saw."

"But he can't row?"

"Yes, he can. I never saw a fellow get into a boat like mine for the first time, and manage himself and the oars as well as he did. He's lived on the Kennebec River, and been in canoes and all sorts of light boats. Just you try him. I'll bet you can't match him for strength in the whole class."

"That's true, I guess," said Minor reflectively.

"And, then," continued Nollie, "he isn't so tied up to tobacco and beer that he'll be likely to give out in the middle of his training just to get back to them."

"To be sure!" said Sine approvingly.

"Then just try him," continued Stavins, earnestly. "I tell you, I'd bet on any thing the most forlorn hope that ever was, if it had him in it. You see, I know him, and you don't."

"Well," said Minor, "I believe we'll put him down for a trial, at any rate. I think that he looks like a promising sort of man myself. But will he agree?"

Nollie had not thought of that. He could not tell. It would certainly be just the exercise John needed, but very likely he would say he could not spare the time. Stavins volunteered, at last, to ask him to come and talk the matter over with the fellows.

By this time Cyril had made his appearance, quite resolved not to accept the place offered him. "I'm sorry, boys," said he, "but I must decline."

"Decline! no such thing: we won't hear of it!"

"Thank you; but you'll have to. There are plenty who will do better than I."

"No: there isn't another one will do as well; you must go."

"But I can not," said Cyril, unusually resolute. "I can not spare the time."

"The time!" said Benson. "Ain't you ashamed to talk of that, when you can get your lessons so easy? Why, man, there's oceans of time! All the time it takes is a little run in the morning, that gets you out early, and is so much clear gain; then a little pull after morning recitation, a little exercise in the gymnasium before dinner, another pull toward evening, and a little run at night again. It don't take more than three hours out of the day. Come, we'll promise you shall have the rest clear. We won't come to your room to bother you, nor tease you to go anywhere. Say you'll pull with us, there's a good fellow!"

"Oh, yes, do, Rivers! you shall! you must!" was echoed round Cyril. It did not move him much, though he was perplexed how to make his fixed resolution evident. Tom's heavy voice at length broke in, silencing the fire of small artillery.

"See here," said he, bringing his tilted chair down upon its four legs, and sitting upright, with a determined expression upon his countenance. "I'm bound this crew shall win, and I'm bound Rivers shall go upon it. Now, I'll make him this offer; and he may accept it or not, just as he has any class-feeling or not. We've got to have a new first-class boat. If Rivers 'll help row it, I'll give the Major a check for five hundred, and he may go down to-morrow, and order just the best that can be built. But, if Rivers won't row, I won't give a cent for the boat. You fellows 'll have to get it up by subscription, the best you can; and the probability is, you won't have it to practice in till within a few days of the race. So there it is, and he may do as he pleases."

There was a thunder of applause in the room at this announcement, — cheers for Raddon, and cries of, "There you are, Rivers!" "Rivers is booked now!" "Hurray for the new boat and glory!" "Hurray for Raddon!"

The tumult dying away, Cyril was found looking pale and agitated. Easy-tempered as he was, there was something in him that rebelled against what looked so like compulsion.

"You don't mean this, Tom?" he said, in an undertone.

"That I do," answered Tom. "I'll swear

to it if you want me to. What do I care for the boat unless you are in it? You can go in and have the sport and the glory as well as not; and, if you won't, they may whistle for their boat."

Cyril stood in silence, trying to overcome his vexation enough to think. Which should he let go, — his personal profit as a student, and as one who sought to get from his time its fullest benefit; or his popularity, his reputation as a man of class-feeling, a good-hearted, generous fellow, ready to join enthusiastically in all that was proposed for the class-glory? The offer of the boat was a great thing. Its cost had laid a heavy expense in prospective upon all interested. To have that so generously given delighted every one, and appeared like an omen of victory. Cyril felt that he could not disappoint the fellows by a churlish refusal of his help. He must give way. The sacrifice would only be for a few weeks. It should not happen again : another year should not pass as this had done.

" Well," said he, as his brow cleared, and

his smile returned, " under such circumstances, I suppose there's only one course for me. I shall have to join the crew and do my best. I'm afraid you've sadly hampered your noble offer, Tom, by making me a condition to it; but there's my hand to promise you I'll do all I can, and thank you for your friendship and your generosity to the class with all my heart."

Tom was more pleased with that little speech, and with the smile upon Cyril's handsome face, than with the applause and gratitude of all the rest. Afterward he said to Cyril, in private, " You got me into college without a condition ; and I told you that was worth an extra five hundred dollars to me this year. It's no more than fair now that you should have the good of it."

" The good of it ! " The words struck even Cyril strangely, since he knew the position into which Tom had, as it were, forced him, was not likely to bring him any good except temporary excitement and pleasure. But neither he nor Tom saw all the meaning in those words. The good of deceit ! the fruit of lies ! What could it be ? What else but ashes and bitterness ? food that was weakness instead of strength, a gain that was poverty, an honor that was shame, a pleasure that was only grief. Such a good poor Tom had, in truth, as he said, offered the friend he really loved, — a reward of hours robbed of their best gifts, of many temptations, of independence exchanged for popular favor. Alas ! Tom, your friendship is oppressive and dangerous. Cyril would not, in honest manly kindness, remove the stumbling-blocks out of your path ; and, all unwittingly, you, in turn, have set snares for his feet. "Whatsoever a man soweth, that shall he also reap."

The noise over the new boat and boatman had hardly subsided, when John Seelye came in with Stavins. It was the first time John had been in so large an informal gathering of his classmates: he was acquainted with but few present, and he did not know why he had been summoned. But he was greeted with respect and cordiality, that gratified the solitary, hard-working man as much as it surprised him. Cyril was deputed to explain why Mr. Seelye had been sent for. He would gladly have remained in the background: his vexation over his broken resolves made him ashamed in the presence of this man, whose respect he had from the first instinctively desired to keep. He knew it was only to himself that his agreement to be upon the crew would seem wrong; but that it did so to himself was enough. There was no way for him, however, but to put the best face upon the matter he was able.

"Mr. Seelye," said he, "we owe you an apology for sending for you so hastily; but we've been choosing a crew for the race, and we want you very much to try taking an oar. Stavins says you know all about pulling; and we think, if you will train with us, you've got just the build and strength to help us win. What do you say? I wish very much you would agree."

He added the last words in all sincerity. Nothing could so have comforted him in his transgression — if the boating was for him a transgression — as the company of upright John Seelye.

The proposition was as delightful to John as it was surprising. Such a token of confidence and friendly feeling from his classmates gratified him exceedingly; and then the prospect of the sport! He seemed, at this minute, to feel the handle of the long oar in his accustomed hands, and to feel the thin, pointed boat shoot forward at the pull of his sturdy arms. He loved the sparkling flow of rivers, the sight of green banks gliding by, the breath of the sweet country air, the freedom of the open heavens overhead. But what did he say? The brightness had not quite vanished from his face, though a little sigh escaped him as he answered.

"There's nothing in the world I like better than rowing, Mr. Rivers; and those wherries and six-oared shells of yours I see on the river would bewitch almost any man who knew what a boat meant. But I can't make one of your crew. Thank you for inviting me, though, all the same."

He showed such a sympathy in the sport in which he denied himself a share, that no one present was willing to accept his refusal. He was overwhelmed with eager entreaties, that astonished and perplexed him. But he was not moved from his decision. To the last "Why can't you?" he answered, —

"You know I came here a poor scholar. But I don't expect to remain so. It will cost me hard work to gain all I mean to, and I can not risk being tempted out of it. That is not all, either," he added, after a short pause, during which his avowal of industrious intentions had made a silence in the room.

"What is it, then?" asked Cyril. He was impelled to ask by a sort of jealousy stirring bitterly in his heart at the sight of one who could be true to his aim. He must know in what more this man's behavior excelled his own. But the rest heard the question too, and waited for the answer.

But John seemed to hesitate about giving it. There was a slight struggle in his mind before he could show such true kindness toward those who had been friendly to him as to express his honest belief when he knew it would be distasteful to them. But, when he did speak, his manner was so pleasant, though fearless, that what he said did not offend, if it did not convince them.

"Why, Mr. Rivers," he said, "I know none of you think as I do; but, to tell the truth, I do not want to train and row for a race. I'd do it for power and speed, but not for victory. A race must be, it can not help but be, a temptation."

"To what?" said Cyril.

"To over-excitement, that's nearly as wicked as drunkenness; to an undue expenditure of thought upon a matter that ought to be always subordinate to our every-day work; to a waste of money the poor world wants for more pressing uses; to ill-feeling; to swearing; to betting; and — yes, even among gentlemen — to cheating."

There was a silence in the room. It was the truth John had spoken: not a man there that did not acknowledge it in his heart.

" What then ? " each asked himself. " Shall we set ourselves to judge and decry the long-established practices of our institution ? be the wise and pious freshmen, whose plea, ' too good to race,' shall make them a singularity, not to say a laughing-stock, in the annals of colleges ? Shall we give up our chance of sport and glory, and that with a new boat and such strong, skillful, enthusiastic men ? Give it all up for a scruple ? Why, no : of course not."

The silence boded no sympathy with John, in his views, from any one. As he rose to go, he said cheerfully, " We can't all think alike, fellows; and, though I've told you what I believe, I never supposed you could all agree to it. But be sure I shall wish for your success in the race just as much as anybody."

As he went away, Nollie Stavins, with a serious face, rose softly and followed him. Cyril looked after them with sorrow in his heart. What a weight and hindrance would have been thrown off his life if just then he had had the manliness to speak out in support of John's opinion, as with his insight and influence he might have done so effectively! But he kept silence, arguing down the noble rebellion in his heart to agreement with the prevailing notions and wishes of those around him.

"What on earth does the fellow mean?" said Tom, as John departed: "that we've no business to race?"

"Exactly," said Benson.

"Well, I declare!" ejaculated Tom. "And he seems like a pretty good fellow too."

"Some of these Down-east fellows have such queer, strict notions!" said another.

"They generally get over 'em after they've been here a while: don't you think so, Rivers?" said Sine.

Cyril shook his head. "No: not when it's like this," said he. "You see," — arguing for himself as well as for the rest, — "there's a basis of truth in what he said. I suppose a race is a temptation; at least, there's always just so much betting and excitement connected with it. But I should say that was not so much the blame of the race as of the way the people not capable of governing themselves go into it. You may make a temptation of every thing if you choose — of eating your dinner every day, for example. No doubt Seelye meant well, and had some ground for his assertion ; but, it seems to me, he would do more good to just enter into the race, and show how a man ought to go through it, than to refuse to have any thing to do with it."

"Never mind, Rivers," said Sine drily: "you and I will do that part for him."

Tom, whose mind had been disturbed by what John said, as by a sort of revelation, threw himself back in his chair with a sort of sigh at this settlement of the question. "Well," said he, "all I know is this : I'm glad I ain't the one to show you all how to enter into temptation. I guess I wasn't cut out for that kind of work."

There was a general laugh. It had a mocking sound to Cyril's ears. Tom's blunt speech had upset all his smooth logic. It was a relief to all when the conversation was turned back to the business of the evening.

The crew was satisfactorily arranged, the new boat was ordered, and the men began training enthusiastically. Cyril entered into the work with as much apparent zeal as if he had not begun it almost upon compulsion. He rose early for his morning row, he ate his rare-beef and oatmeal cakes, took his regular rest and exercise with as much precision and as much seeming sense of the importance of all this painstaking as any of his comrades. But there was that in his mind which merry Benson and Minor, their hearts set upon the attainment of their object, not upon estimating its value, never knew. It was a half-heeded, regretful questioning as to the use of the effort, an occasional passing feeling of scorn at sight of his companions innocently but so earnestly discussing the question whether they might drink two gills or a pint of water, or whether it would do to use butter and milk with their oatmeal porridge. Was the end worth all this thought about eating and sleeping, and all this endurance, this forcing one's self to a routine, whatever the mood, or the varying calls of the day, so that a man must run when the clear morning brain made the aspect of books beautiful, and go through grim pulling of weights in a gymnasium when his heart was drawn to social converse with friends upon the benches under the elms outside?

Cyril did not miss the fact that it is a good thing for a man to know that he may keep himself a bond-slave to his purpose. And let me say here, that, in describing his feelings about this matter, no one need suppose I would condemn such a course of training as he had entered upon. It must be of inestimable and life-long value to many: it is all that has appeared to redeem the purpose for which it is undertaken. But I condemn Cyril for entering upon it because he knew in his heart it was not for him — whatever it might be to others — the most profitable exercise to which he could give his time. The unworthy motives, so exciting to some, and kept so constantly in view, often, in his secret heart, disquieted him. "That a man," he would think to himself, "with all the possibilities the days hold for him, should give himself up to his conversion into a race-horse!" There were moments when it seemed to Cyril that all his fellows were governed by a puerile infatuation, an ambition that might have been expected only in barbarians. But that was all hidden deep in his heart: it never came to light.

Like the rest, Cyril gave himself up for two months to become a " good oar; " slept and ate for that; went in and came out for that; talked and read about that; and, like the rest, did not advance much in learning any thing but that. His face grew brown; and all its softness and roundness disappeared in a hard, spare look, the skin drawn closely over the muscles and swollen veins, giving him an expression of strained hardihood, such as some weather-beaten, much-enduring pioneer or soldier might exhibit. His shoulders grew broad, and his arms powerful. But his mind seemed to lose something of fire and vitality as his body gained. It might have been because of the tax upon his strength, and it might have been because his attention was **so diverted** from his studies, that he often felt a certain restlessness and impatience when he would **have devoted** himself to his book. And then he was **so** pressed for time. Be sure if you lay upon the limited table of your day **all** the occupations it **will hold,** another's thoughtless hand, or your **own eager one, will,** before long, attempt **to crowd in** something more ; and then **some part** of **the legitimate burden** is displaced, — pushed on to another **day as** well-filled **as the** first, — and so, perhaps, never finds **a** place. It is better to have a margin, lest, in trying **to do all** that **we** might, we fail to do all that **we** ought. Cyril had completely filled up his time with exercise **and** study, hoping to make room **for all** he seemed called upon to do. But now he was surprised to find how entirely he failed to carry out his arrangements. His training went on well enough, to be sure, for that was now **the** first consideration. **But his** study-hours were constantly **broken in** upon. The row or the **run** would last a little longer than **it** ought. It would be necessary to linger a while at the boat-house to watch the upper-class men coming in or going out, so as to compare progress; or he would be detained in interesting conversation about the prospect of the race. Many a time he found himself running to recitation at the last toll of the bell, with the unsatisfactory knowledge that the three minutes he had dared to linger could not make up for the thirty lost before the lesson was begun.

Under these circumstances you will not be surprised to find Cyril soon freely using the dishonest help he had not discountenanced for others, but which he had once scorned to rely upon himself. Benson's "ponies" found their way to Cyril's study-table; and even that dirty manuscript-book of corrected Greek exercises, that Tom had purchased from a sophomore, and that was handed about for copying among the idlest, most unprincipled men in the class, Cyril did not now refuse to avail himself of. It was only for a while, he said, and there was no other way. The day set for the races was drawing near; the zeal of the boatmen and the excitement of their friends and abettors were increasing with the summer heat. There was nothing but hurry and dissipation of mind. He was uneasy at his course sometimes. All the lessons passed by in those weeks were in the retrospect like haunting, unfeatured ghosts, every one pointing to the day of examination. He remembered with a blush of shame, too, Tom's speech about entering into temptation. Ah! how Cyril had failed to show himself one who could endure it! And yet he could argue out some comfort: others were more faulty than he; they all thought him remarkably faithful to study; two or three times he had refused to join the crew in plans to "cut" recitation, when they aspired to more practice than there was time for. Why need he be for ever blaming himself for what others were doing without the least compunction?

Alas, Cyril! rather ask why you should stand drawing comparisons between yourself and others more ignorant. Cease to glance over the surface of your days, filling your ears with their thousand voices of temptation, and your eyes with their fleeting lights of allurement, and come back to behold the truth of your life, and to hear the decrees of duty in the depths of your soul. In all these little errings, you will find great transgressions. Your carelessness in study is only for three or four weeks, you say. Yes; but in those weeks you have cheated your father of the price of his earnest toil. Are you not bound to gain the utmost from the privilege he is straining his powers to the utmost to afford you? It was no mere smattering he sent you here to gain, no merely civilizing process, not simply a polite familiarity with classic names and languages. It was thorough culture, the habit of patient labor and thought, the mastery and the enlightened use of your powers, so that in your middle life no one can look sadly upon you and say, " He is not the man, that, with the best development of his faculties, he might have become."

I know you have written to him, and told him of your new engagements, and of some of the things that have been crowded out of your day; and he wrote you back no word of rebuke, — only sympathy in your efforts, and cheerful wishes for your success. He did not tell you that he sighed a little over your letter, that it cost him a little struggle with some vague anxiety and disappointment, before he could write that kind reply. But he could not bear to have you think he did not trust you. He was always over-fond and proud of you. He argued to himself that the thing was innocent, that it was never in the nature of youth to be able to resist the charms of physical sports; and, no doubt, that was to them a blessing and protection. But, because of his indulgence, is your debt to him any the less binding?

The day of the races came at last. Since it is natural to sympathize most with those whom we know best, perhaps you will be sorry to hear that it closed in disappointment to the freshmen. Their failure was, no doubt, owing to their want of experience in such matters. Their splendid boat and good training had given them a fair prospect of success. They started well, and soon outstripped their natural enemies, the sophs., and then the lazy, half-in-earnest juniors. But they could not match the well-practiced and matured strength of the senior crew. They pulled desperately to gain upon them ; but, after a while, finding themselves, instead, losing inch by inch, they became a little demoralized by despair : insensibly their efforts were weakened, they seemed to have no reserve of strength, and, at last, even suffered the boat behind them to get by and come in ahead.

Well, it was a hard thing for them to come in beaten and mortified, — to find Tom Raddon and others angrily swearing over their disappointment and their lost bets; to receive the condolence of those more philosophical, and to see how crest-fallen were all their lately exultant classmates. Benson actually flung himself upon the floor of the boat-house, and cried for vexation. Minor, pale with anger, without opening his lips to friend or foe, stalked away to his room, and was there sick for a week. Cyril bore the defeat a little more manfully, did his best to comfort the mourning, spoke cheerily, and argued from to-day at least certain victory next year.

But, in the following days, he felt the reaction almost as overwhelmingly as the others. He seemed thoroughly wretched; mortification that was very much like remorse was in his mind, and languor in his overstrained body. He felt little inclined to make the most of the two short weeks that lay between him and examination; but then his carelessness in the days past made him anxious about those to come. He was not reconciled to the thought that his stand at the end of the first year must fall far below that he held on entering. He was urged to do all that he could in the short time remaining. He was glad, too, to shut out the throng of companions, whose faces had, for a while, grown tiresome to him. He closed his door, therefore, as willfully as he was able, and, battling with the distaste for application that vexed his mind, set himself to work in earnest. He soon discovered how much more he had lost than he had supposed possible. He studied desperately all day and late into the night, in the sudden change from his late regular habits trifling dangerously with the strength of his constitution. It was a wonder that he endured to the close of the term without serious illness.

If the result of the examination was humbling to the expectations he had cherished earlier in his college life, he hardened his heart to the fact. There was many a fine fellow who would still be glad to rank as high as he. Yet no one congratulated him, and he could not congratulate himself; for he could not hide from himself the fact that he had not done as well as many of his friends expected. But it would be a happy thing for him if that failure in scholarship was the worst he had made in his first year at college.

CHAPTER V.

THE MISSION SCHOOL.

" Behold, thou . . . . makest thy boast of God;

" And knowest his will, and approvest the things that are more excellent, being instructed out of the law.

" Thou, therefore, which teachest another, teachest thou not thyself ? "

THE long vacation was over. There was a new bustle in the streets of Eaton, as though the old city had just waked from a siesta in the noon of the year. So much young life received again into her bosom, all restless after two months' liberty, and with animal spirits at their highest in the beautiful autumn weather, must make her feel a change. The very elms overhead seemed to sway with livelier breezes, and to take on a brighter yellow in the sunshine. To-day, the first Sabbath in October, the old chapel-bell, for some time silent, once more joined its peal with the rest, great and small, from the steeples of the town; and its voice of compulsion, that spared the ears of neither the profane nor the slothful, has gathered in once more the restless congregation of young men.

It is noon now; and, while many have dispersed, some still remain in the chapel to partake of the Lord's Supper, administered at this hour. The little band are more decorous in attitude, more thoughtful in expression, than the audience here usually appears: if there are among them those who sometimes thoughtlessly sleep or play in church as irreligious companions do, they are now, at least, subdued and serious and penitent.

If we look here for old friends, we shall find Cyril Rivers and John Seelye. John's hard face, browned by the summer sun, is worth noticing just now, it is so softened and ennobled in its expression by his earnest devotion. Cyril looks more than a year older than when we first met him: the brightness and confidence his face used to show are subdued by a touch of melancholy and by some inward experience of humiliation. He has come from home with his old aims in some measure revived, but with a better knowledge of the struggle it must cost him to be true to them. He has come with some sorrow, too, for the shortcomings of which the past year was so full. Shall we analyze this gentle regret, born of affection to father and friends, and of the perception of what gratitude demands from him, and of what he owes himself, and seek in it a graver sadness, because of the heavenly Father whose service he had slighted and forgotten? Surely, at this first hour, when Cyril has come back to his table to feed at his hand, such a grief can not be entirely wanting in the young man's heart. Else why is his face so troubled at the time when of all others it should be shining with joy and peace?

That unusual look of sadness at the close of the service attracted John Seelye's attention. His heart was full of love just then, and it was drawn out toward Cyril. He remembered how often they had sat near each other at the communion, without coming any nearer in friendly acquaintance ; and he bethought himself of how many temptations must beset this younger brother, from the throng of flattering companions about him, and from a heart responsive to the voice of every pleasure, not chastened by labor and care like his own. With a good thought in his mind, John quickened his steps so as to overtake Cyril.

What he had to say was soon explained. He was engaged in teaching in a mission Sunday school in the city, where one of the tutors had taken him upon his first coming to college. More teachers were wanted there ; and John asked Cyril to go with him this noon, and see the school, and perhaps take a class. Cyril was a minister's son, and brought up in Sunday-school work: teaching was easy for him, with his natural gift for speaking attractively, and his familiarity with Bible truths. In his present half homesick, wholly self-sick state of mind, the proposition was very welcome. Going in good company to do good work promised to soothe the ache which his conscience, roused

to its wounds, was keeping up in his heart. It
would be far pleasanter to spend the noon so
than in his room, where, if he tried to read, he
would be interrupted by classmates lounging
in to while away the tedious hours with unprofitable if not profane conversation. He
acceded to John's request very gladly.

The school was upon the outskirts of the
city, in a forlorn region, built up with the un-
lovely dwellings of the poor. Here private
charity had erected a little chapel-building,
made its plain interior as attractive as might be,
with texts and colored letters upon the walls,
hanging-baskets of flowers and evergreens, and
pictures of Scripture scenes. Here were gathered a hundred or more children from the
neighborhood. They were shabbily attired,
and their very faces, alas! rank after rank of
them, bore testimony to the certainty of the
law that the little ones were learning to repeat,
" visiting the iniquity of the fathers upon the
children, to the third and fourth generation of
them that hate me." Here was presented the
sad sight of a childhood without beauty.

Even if by chance you find among the rest some little Marian Erle, whom suffering has purified, her thin and pallid cheeks, her large and eager eyes, are too pitiful to be pleasing. Here are faces whose hue shows how the whole body languishes for cleanliness and pure air, — faces that you gaze upon dissatisfied and regretful, puzzled with searching for something which should be in them, and is not, or with wondering at that which is in them, and should not be; faces that would be beautiful, if — if not for that unduly developed feature, perhaps, or that premature look, or that sensual or sly or dull or fierce expression. Ah! when we go down from a happier lot, and look upon those born in ignorance and sin, and wonder to find them so far from our standard of beauty, let us think, that with such sorrow and disappointment, because of the grace and glory which we should wear and do not, God and the angels take knowledge of us. Methinks we are all only poor, careless, ignorant, half-listening children in God's mission-school; and not all the glory and the beauty of the temple he has built for us, not all the heavenly love and sweet plead-ing of the chief Shepherd he has put over us, can win from us more than a weak trust, a fickle obedience, a wavering attention.   With what long-suffering patience, then, with what all-trusting, all-hoping charity, shall not we, who are ourselves such ungrateful, erring schol-ars, be exercised toward the little ones put in our charge ?

Cyril looked about upon the school; and his heart, susceptible to what was fine in the spirit of any scene, was soothed and pleased.   When the opening exercises were over, he was given the charge of a turbulent class of large boys, newly drawn into the school.   There was scope enough to use all his powers of pleasing, and to prove himself a master of influence in keeping them in order, to say nothing of instructing them.   There was fresh pleasure to him, then, in finding that the something in him which had attracted Tom Raddon and others did not fail in its effect upon these boys.   They were quiet under the gentle tone of Cyril's voice.   His ready insight into their nature and ways of

CYRIL WITH HIS SABBATH SCHOOL CLASS.

thought, and his talent for illustration, and versatility of expression, enabled **him to put** what he **had to** say into such shape **that they** would listen to **it** and remember **it. It was** only a **short half-hour that he had to** talk to them **; but in that time he** contrived **to** establish **a friendly footing** between them and himself, so that at **the close of** the lesson they asked him if he would come again. He was willing enough to promise. He enjoyed, more than any thing, **his** conquests in winning love. The **sadness with** which he had left church had departed, **and** left him self-content and happy. But the scene, **and the exercise in which he** had taken part, **had** excited all his religious and poetic emotions, and set his mind working with many **thoughts.** They were not thoughts of himself, **sorrowful and** condemnatory ; yet, by some impulse of the wishful, struggling angel in his soul, they **were** of that which he ought to be and was the farthest from being. As **the** thirsty traveler in the desert beholds **a** mirage **of fair** waters, so his spirit was imaging forth, with a delusive, temporary gratification, as if it were enough merely to be able to see, the beauty of that state it was least likely to attain. He was not sorry that the superintendent, attracted by his looks and the apparent enthusiasm with which he had thrown himself into the work of the hour, after a short consultation with John, asked him if he would make a short address to the children before the close of the school.   There were some words that had been read at the opening that had been shining before his mind ever since; and the thoughts that had arisen about these words, because there was an audience about him, had put themselves into the shape of discourse to that audience, It was often so in Cyril's mind : the instinct of expression was so strong, that his ideas, as they came to his own consciousness, oftener presented themselves in the form of dialogue or address than in any other way.   Therefore, he went up very readily to the speaker's platform ; and when he stood there, and looked around upon the children, there was that brightness in his eye, and earnestness upon his face, that showed him to be at no loss for subject-matter of discourse.

When his glance had drawn all eyes upon his own, he suddenly raised them, as if looking away through the low roof into the heaven of heavens. "Children," he said, while all the wondering glances followed his, "I am thinking of that wonderful vision of which we have read to-day : I seem to see it now, — I can not forget the words of it." He paused a moment, and then slowly, and with great intensity and force, as if he were indeed the seer, began to repeat the following : —

" ' And I saw heaven opened ; and, behold, a white horse ; and he that sat upon him was called Faithful and True, and in righteousness he doth judge and make war !

" ' His eyes were as a flame of fire ; and on his head were many crowns ; and he had a name written that no man knew but he himself. And he was clothed with a vesture dipped in blood ; and his name is called the Word of God.

" ' And the armies which were in heaven followed him upon white horses, clothed in fine linen, white and clean.' "

His tone and manner were such that the eyes of his audience were fastened upon him with a strained gaze, as though they saw with his vision, and little faces fairly grew pale with solemnity and wonder.

"Do you think," he continued, "that sight is something far-off and wonderful, — something you will see many years after death, when you have gone from this to other worlds?

"No: I tell you it is the story of what has begun now. Who is this upon the white steed of victory, with the many crowns, the eyes of fire, the garment dipped in blood? It is Jesus Christ, who was slain upon earth, but who was raised from death, and has come again a conqueror. By faith we may see him now, riding through all the earth upon his white steed. His eyes of fire search all hearts, and many kings call him their Lord. By the story that his blood-stained garments tell, the story of how he died to take away our sins, the story of his love to all men, and by his word in the Bible, and his Holy Spirit in the hearts of men, he is subduing the whole earth to himself.

" And who are these, the armies of heaven, mounted like him, conquering with him, clothed in clean linen, pure and white ? Why, you need not wait till death to see their bright array ! They are about you everywhere : they are the good men and women who labor for him, who love him, whom he has made his servants, and equipped for the war with his own hand. He has put on them the white robe of his own righteousness, and set them on his strong white steeds of grace and redemption.

" Will you come, children, and join this train ? Would you have the Conqueror help you to become strong and joyful servants ? and would you help him win the victory ? He wants you in his army : he has called you to-day, by the teachers who have told you of his warfare and his glory. And I will tell you how you may join his ranks. Not by going to another world, or to other work than you do every day now. But let each one of you say to himself earnestly now, ' If he will help me, I will follow him ; ' and instantly the angel of God will write his name on the roll-call of that great army.

"But his soldiers must be as he is. His name is Faithful and True: they must bear it. You must try to make it yours. You must be faithful and true, — faithful to his commandments, faithful in honoring him, faithful in praying to him and in working for him, faithful all day long, and every hour, and to the end of your life. And then you must be true, — true in the words of your mouth and the thoughts of your heart; true in every action and appearance. You must strive to be so, and beg him to make you so.

"And then his soldiers must take up his work. What is it? 'In righteousness to judge and make war.' Your work is not all like his; for he is to judge men, — you and me and the whole earth. You are to judge only yourselves, your own thoughts and actions, — to judge all day long what is right and what is wrong for yourself; to judge what pleasures you must not have, what hard tasks you must call your duty, what wishes you must deny. And then you are to make war, — to make war against sin everywhere; war against all lying and Sabbath-breaking and profanity and intemperance and covetousness. You are not too young nor too feeble to begin it. Do not wait, delaying and looking about for your steeds of strength and your shining garments : God will supply them before you are aware. Only trust him for that, and begin and follow him. Do what little things you can for him every day : keep remembering him, and waiting to serve him. He will give you greater and greater strength, and greater and greater deeds to do for him ; and when he does visibly come in glory with the armies of heaven, surely your names shall be numbered in their ranks."

The words were true and well-spoken. Perhaps they sank deep in some tender minds, half-comprehended, but to be held tenaciously and revolved in thought again and again, till the growing soul is able to grasp their meaning. Perhaps the earnest manner in which they were said has inspired a belief in things unseen in hearts never lifted above sight and sense before. But alas for the speaker!

Alas for him who teaches and can not follow his own teaching! for him who, taught in the law, through breaking the law dishonors God! O Cyril! where are your faith and truth? Where is the watchful judgment you are daily passing upon your heart and life? Where is the stern yet kindly warfare that you are earnestly waging?

Perhaps it may seem impossible to some that thoughts like these to which I have described Cyril as giving expression could take possession, even temporarily, of a man's mind, and yet have no influence upon his life. But it is a favorite device of Satan's to flatter a man upon his mere perception of the truth, so that in his complacency over his wisdom he forgets to carry it into action. The hearer of the word deceives himself, and fails to become a doer of it. Just as Cyril did, he beholds himself, and goes his way, and straightway forgets what manner of man he is.

At the close of the school, Cyril found among the teachers a young lady whom he had previously met, — a pleasant, lively girl, who was evidently pleased to claim acquaintance with him, and who introduced him to some of her companions. In their company, engaged in lively conversation, he walked back to church. His old happy, self-complacent frame of mind had returned : not a trace was left of the regret and dissatisfaction he had brought from home, and carried in greater or less weight till now. In talking to the children, he seemed to have thrown off the thoughts of duty that had oppressed him ; and, for a season, they vexed him no more.

He sat in church, his mind running more upon the little incidents of the afternoon, and the conversation of the young ladies, than upon the sermon to which he seemed to be listening. He went to his room, to be followed by Raddon and Benson and others, who would commence talking over vacation experiences. When the conversation waxed altogether too noisy or profane, Cyril would try to quiet it by such tact as he was master of. But he did not make honest war upon it, as Seelye would have done, showing its unsuitableness to holy time,

and setting himself to win them all to some
better occupation. There lay the Bible, hardly
more familiar to Tom than if he had been
born a Buddhist or a Brahmin ; and there were
the books of comment Cyril's father had desired him to study, to help him discover the
depth of the riches of wisdom contained in its
pages. What if he had chosen to ask those
who loved him to study it with him at that
hour ? Might there not have been something
to have laid hold upon their interest in the
lives of Gideon and Samson and Barak, of
Jephtha and of David, — those lives that had
struggled between the depravity of the natural
heart and the aspirations of the spiritual, till
the victory was given them by faith ? Was
there nothing that could have pleased Cyril and
his friends, — nothing they needed to contemplate in the tale of that Young Man who early
was filled with the thoughts of his Father's
business ; who was holy, harmless, undefiled ;
who pleased not himself ; who gave his life, at
last, a ransom for many ? Why, Cyril, why
have you not more of the spirit of him whom

you profess to follow ?   It was not all with him to draw to himself the love of publicans and sinners, but through that love to lift their thoughts with his away from earth to heaven. If your course is not set so firmly that your companions must needs follow it with you or cease to be your companions, then must they draw you into their way, as they are doing at this hour.

After tea that Sunday evening, Nollie Stavins came and asked Cyril to go with him to church.   But, before they started, Tom entered the room.   He wanted the solution of such problems in to-morrow's lessons as he could not at once understand.   Cyril, though well acquainted with his ways, and without any hope of inducing him to change them, nevertheless lightly reminded him that it was Sunday night, and that he could not help him make such "a heathen" of himself as to get his lessons now.

"Get my lessons!" said Tom roughly. "If you're concerned about my heathenism, you'd better be glad it's only that.   It's the decentest thing I've done to-day, except going to chapel because they made me; and, if it wasn't for these problems, I should be down at Toby's rolling billiards this minute! You needn't look shocked!" he continued, seeing that both Cyril and Nollie looked disturbed at this reminder of his bad habits: there are different ways for different people. You were brought up among the saints, and it's easy for you to go to church and be saints; but I was brought up among the heathen, and I have to be a heathen and go play billiards."

To this statement of destiny, Cyril said nothing: perhaps he half accepted it. But Stavins's face flushed with earnestness. "There are different kinds of people, Tom, and brought up in different ways," he said: "but there is only one commandment for all from God; and that is, 'Remember the Sabbath day to keep it holy.'"

Cyril would, by instinct, have spoken the words more gently, — not so rebukingly, — so that they would not have ruffled Tom, while they convicted him. But Cyril, take notice, did not speak them at all.

Tom scowled and looked vexed. After a minute, he declared gruffly, that, commandment or no, he must have those problems to-night. " Will you let me take yours, Rivers," he said, " or must I go chasing round to get Sine, or somebody else, to do me such a little favor ? "

Cyril reluctantly reached the papers upon which he had worked out his problems, and put them in Tom's hand. " It's no use," he said, in an undertone, excusing himself to Stavins : " he'll do it any way; and there's no chance to keep any influence over him at all except to show one's self friendly."

" I wish you wouldn't study to-night, Tom," he said seriously ; " but do promise one thing, at any rate, and that is, when you get through with these, not to go down to ' Toby's.' You know he keeps that saloon open Sunday nights contrary to law; and the police are likely to be down upon it any time. If you fellows are found there you'll be sent straight out of college. Keep away from there, Tom, to-night, at any rate."

" Hang it all ! " said Tom, as he hastily took

the papers and turned away: "do you think I don't know there's a risk? That's half the fun in this slow place."

Cyril's effort was made in worldly wisdom, and it produced not the least effect; Stavins had spoken in genuine zeal for truth, and his words, too, seemed to have failed of any result. But, in reality, they were still uppermost in Tom's mind. "One commandment for all! one commandment for all!" he muttered to himself; "and that when it would be so hard for me to be like them!" At every interval of his work, the words returned to his thought and made him restless and uneasy. He did not go to the billiard saloon that night, but it was not the fear of the officers of the law that kept him away.

CHAPTER VI.

THE READY WRITER.

"The righteous man falling down before the wicked is as a
troubled fountain and a corrupt spring."

CYRIL continued his attendance
at the Sunday school. There was
much to attract him there. His
going soothed his conscience after a
week of selfish occupations, without any
thought of the service of God. The tokens of
love and confidence he won from his class, and
the signs of his influence over them, were a
perpetual and ever-new source of pleasure to
him. Their improvement in conduct and appearance was noticed by others in the school
besides himself. It was owing, no doubt, not
so much to what he taught them as to their
admiration of the teacher, and their natural
imitation of him. He was to them a revela-

tion of a life possessed of powers and pleasures greater than they could have dreamed of; and he offered them, in himself, a model easier to see and copy than the Great One he had been set to show forth to them.

Besides the pleasures his class gave him, the teachers of the school, co-operating in the conduct of its affairs, afforded him society of the pleasantest kind, because it was a society enlivened by and interested in the joint prosecution of a useful work. Its meetings had business that concerned every member, and drew out the best thoughts and pleasantest characteristics of each, bringing about a very agreeable kind of converse. Moreover, Cyril soon found himself as great a favorite in these gatherings as he was elsewhere. He was so full of spirits, and such a quick-witted and graceful speaker, that his way was always the popular way.

Cyril had begun this year with renewed ambition as a student. He began well, and for the first few weeks rose rapidly in scholarship, and fought manfully to keep clear of outside engagements, that thick and fast crowded to claim his attention. But, through his friends in·college and in the Sunday school, he had made an extended and pleasant acquaintance among the livelier society of the place; and from that quarter, as well as from the solicitations of his fellow-students, temptations were continually offering themselves. One day, early in the winter, he received an invitation to attend a set of sociables. They were to meet fortnightly at the pleasantest houses in town, and to offer various entertainments, charades and tableaux, music and dancing. The young lady who detailed this delightful plan to Cyril was sure that he would be a most invaluable assistant in the gayety, and had, moreover, been instructed by the clique of friends with whom she was acting to say that he must on no account refuse his attendance and co-operation. It did not need her earnest effort to make the plan appear attractive to Cyril, with his lively imagination and social tastes; yet she could not, with all her pretty coaxing, persuade him to give his consent to it at once. He was evidently sincere in saying how much her plan attracted him; but he declared he must have time to consider it, and that she must not be surprised if he refused it. He urged his studies, and the pressure of many other engagements upon his time, as his excuse, and left her admiringly impressed, not only with his good looks and pleasant manners, but his devotion to duty, and steadfastness in resisting temptation.

But it was all a mistake. Cyril was not thinking of his duty at all. It offered him a good ground for withdrawal when he did not like to tell the truth, which was, that he could not bear the slight expenses such entertainments must entail upon him. He had in many unexpected ways, not wantonly, but as it seemed almost by necessity, strained his father's bounty to its utmost limits: he had found, since coming to college, so many more wants, and they had been so much more costly than he had anticipated. He knew he could not ask even for a very little more money. He was willing to wear the best suit he had, though it was rather worn and past the style; but then there were the etcæteras, — white gloves, fresh neck-ties, shoes more suitable than his rough walking-boots. There was the occasional necessity to pay carriage-fare for ladies, and all the little incidental expenses with which society charges its favorites, which Cyril had experience enough to know were constant and inevitable. He had been caught by them before: they always counted lightly in the first place, but in the end were sure to amount to what, to a man whose every dollar was spared him for some necessary purpose, would, at least, be a matter of consideration.

The more Cyril thought over the invitation, the more he was tempted; and the more he was tempted, the more the want of means perplexed and baffled him. One evening he sat in his room writing a composition. He was a fluent and able writer for his years, — so ingenious he never failed for argument, so well-read he always had facts and illustrations in proof, and so imaginative that his pages never lacked the ornaments of fancy.

Writing was an easy task to him, but he liked to take pains with it. The subject this time was one for debate; and Cyril, to please himself, had written down all the arguments he could think of upon the most favorable side of the question, and then, with the utmost ingenuity, answered them, one after another, in the essay he meant to read in the class. He was engaged in putting the finishing touches to this essay — which would be called for to-morrow morning — when Tom Raddon came to his room. Tom groaned aloud when he saw the papers upon Cyril's desk. Cyril understood him with the vexed solicitude of a careful older brother over a careless, stupid, younger one.

"Haven't you done your essay, Raddon?" he asked.

"Hang it, no!" said Tom.

It was Cyril's turn to groan now. "You said you'd do it in season this once," he said.

"I know it; but how could I? There hasn't been a minute's time, if I'd had oceans, instead of nothing whatever, to say. I might as well fail again, I suppose: I've flunked every lesson, so far, right through the week."

" You can't go on in this way much longer," said Cyril.

Tom muttered, that, as there could not be a worse way, perhaps it was a good thing that he could not. Cyril cast about for some motive that would have weight in remonstrating with him.

" Don't you ever think of the future, Tom ? " he asked. " I thought you were here to prepare yourself for political life."

" So my father said," answered Tom recklessly: " and I guess he was right; for all the politicians, as far as I can see, are about as proficient in billiards and mixed drinks as any thing else."

Cyril was vexed. " Stop talking like a fool, Raddon," he said quite sharply. " Why can't you listen to reason? you know it's time you did."

Such a tone was so unusual for him that it did not anger Tom, only sobered him. He had such a genuine affection for this friend, that, when he saw him really vexed and disturbed, he was sorry. He looked, in a moment, curiously humble, subdued, and serious.

"Yes: it's time, Rivers," he said. "I will listen. Do, if you can, talk a little reason to me, and a little — what do you call it? — a little conscience too. I guess I need it."

There was in his mind at that moment some good longing for vital instruction. If Cyril had been living an earnest life himself, so that his mind had been full of earnest thoughts, here would have been the golden opportunity for speaking them. Tom, whom he had supposed ignorant of the very existence of such a thing, had asked him to speak of conscience. But there was nothing in Cyril's heart which prompted him to make the right use of the moment. He failed his friend miserably.

"You almost never study, Tom," he said. "You waste your time awfully. If you don't look out, you'll be dropped from the class at the end of this year; and you told me that when your father sent you here, he said if he found out you did not show yourself as smart as the rest of us at your books, he would cut you off without a shilling. I say you've got to change your course."

"Oh, yes, confound it! but how can I?" said Tom, somehow disappointed to hear again the same old story of caution that Cyril was so often telling. "You've said it a thousand times, and I know it as well as you; but that does not do any good."

"Well, you've got to *do* something about it!" said Cyril. "Just cut that lazy crowd you are going with, and begin to work."

"But I've tried it three times this term, I tell you, and it's no use. The fellows won't let me alone. Besides, when I work like a horse, I don't seem to make any headway with my lessons. And, confound it all, what is life worth if you've got to work like a drudge through the very best part of it? I tell you, I never shall have such years, nor such good fellowship, again in this world as I have here now; and I'll enjoy them while I have them. My father needn't expect I shall do otherwise."

Where were Cyril's reasons of worldly wisdom and prudence now ?   Tom had out-argued them.   If we live for pleasure and the gratifi- cation of selfishness, surely it is best to snatch them now, when youth and health, and the shining present, make them most fresh and de- lightful.   Cyril sat in silence, discomfited to see how powerless his earnestness had proved.

"But you haven't made up your mind to fail utterly ?" he said, at last.   "You've got some ambition left.   Can't you see how these things would help you ?   This debate-writing, now : you ought to practice it voluntarily, in- stead of shirking it.   If you won't climb the steps to your profession, you'll never reach it."

"Well, I did try in earnest on those things," said Tom ; "and, to judge from the results, I should think I was the last man to make a writer or a speaker.   There wasn't a line old M'Tafor didn't correct.   The grammar was wrong, and the spelling was wrong, and even the ideas, he said, were inexcusably mistaken and wrong.   Then we've had such subjects ! I didn't know any more about them than about the moon.   How could I write about them ?"

" Why don't you hunt up a little information?" said Cyril.

" There's no time. The hours go off like smoke, and I don t know where they go to. They've all gone this week, and this talk won't help me to-morrow."

" Here's paper and ink," said Cyril: "begin and write something now."

" But I haven't the first idea what to write. How do I know whether ' liberty or law is the best educator'?"

Cyril was perplexed. He had no mind to go into such an explanation of the subject as would awaken Tom's interest and thought about it; but some such talk seemed imposed upon him if he would save his friend a failure. He was thinking how he should throw into condensed form the main thoughts upon the subject for Tom's benefit, when the latter saved him the trouble. Tom had drawn his chair to the table, and was idly turning over the papers that lay upon it, when he came upon Cyril's rough draught of the arguments to be refuted in his essay.

"What's this?" said Tom, as he began reading it aloud; "not your essay?"

"No: only a statement of the other side of the question."

"But it's good enough for an essay, — better than the best I could write. It just helps me out of my scrape. Sell it to me, Rivers. I'll give you two dollars for it."

"No: I don't want to sell it," said Cyril, much vexed. "You can't have it: M'Tafor would know at once it wasn't yours."

"He wouldn't," said Tom; "and, if he did, how could he prove it? Besides, I'll fix it up. I begin to see what it all means, now I've read this. I'll have a composition that can't be beat. I shall send it for my father to read. He'll think I'm the greatest man going. Just hand me that pen, old fellow."

Tom never seemed to see any reason why he should not seize what he wanted, whatever objections were made. Cyril's feeble remonstrances he cast away like the wind; and Cyril was too much in the habit of yielding to him to make any very determined resistance. Cyril did not want the paper; and, though he had not voluntarily accepted it, yet he did want the money Tom had offered for the purchase. He could not help it, he said to himself, if Tom chose to cheat himself and his teacher. Tom had got the paper in his hands now, and would not give it up again. Perhaps, after all, it would not give him more help than Cyril must have done by talking with him about the subject.

So Cyril allowed Tom to get paper and ink, and begin copying the abstract of arguments. He wrote it in a sprawling handwriting, which made the matter upon two lines of Cyril's manuscript extend half-way down the page of his own. That was a trick of self-deception brought with him out of childhood, by which he once fancied, and perhaps even yet fancied, his composition would appear the longer for taking up the more space upon paper. But, having caught from what he wrote some interest in its meaning, he soon began interpolating ideas of his own; and Cyril saw him biting his nails and rubbing his hair into confusion, in

the effort to bring his thoughts to expression.
There was silence in the room while he worked.
Cyril finished his own work and put it away.
The quiet satisfaction which he had felt about
it before Tom came in was destroyed.   He
was disturbed in heart.   He took a book, and
tried to read, but his mind wandered.   He
must needs think of Tom.   He wondered why
it was, that, because the fellow followed him and
hung upon him, he must feel an irksome sense
of responsibility for Tom.   He had not sought
his friendship in the first place: why must he
feel guilty at the thought of Tom's getting
into trouble and disgrace?   Why did he care
any thing about him? and especially why must
he feel that he ought to care for him much
more than he had ever done; be kinder to him,
yet severer with him; do more for him, yet
deny him more, cultivate his friendship, yet
resist his ideas?   Cyril had done violence to
this feeling many times, but he could not now
dismiss it from his mind.   There was trouble in
his conscience on Tom's account that he could
not reason away.   No wonder it was so.

Those whose affection God gives us he in a manner lays upon us : their safety and welfare are, to a certain extent, our charge. Does he give us influence over any one, he will call us to account for the power. Have we been too indolent or inefficient to exercise it, or have we done so only to amuse and gratify ourselves, one day we shall be called to confess and to mourn over the misused or buried talent. Nay, the puuishment will not wait till that day. It begins with the sin. The clinging object that we will not lift up with us toward heaven will draw us down to the earth by its own weight.

If Cyril caught a glimpse of this truth as he sat musing over the unheeded pages of his book, he did not try to obtain a nearer view. From Tom and his writing his mind soon wandered to pleasanter themes. There lay the two-dollar note that Tom, asking no consent but his own to the exchange, had laid down in place of the essay. How strange it seemed, Cyril thought, that one should throw his money about like that! No doubt Tom would almost forget he had paid it, just as, having paid it, and so, as he supposed, made the essay entirely his own, he would almost forget he had not originated every word of that. But that note now represented to Cyril the white gloves that helped make Miss Kerlie's sociable possible to him. His mind wandered to thoughts of that bright-eyed young lady, and of the pleasures she had planned, and the flattering desire she had so urgently expressed to have him take part in them.

His self-complacency was restored. In the midst of many pleasing visions, his mind soon ran astray, vanity getting the mastery of it. So that at last, when, toward twelve o'clock, Tom held up his finished composition, saying, " There, old fellow, I'm gloriously fixed for to-morrow; and thank you for it!" Cyril answered from the midst of his dreams, " You needn't, Tom : at that price " — pointing to the note — " I'd like to write compositions for the whole division."

O Cyril! how could you say it without shame ? Think what it is that you propose to cover your hands with, that they may be spotless enough to offer to gentle ladies! It is the price of a lie! It should seem to you that the whitest gloves bought with that money would turn black upon your palms, and that any true hand would instinctively draw back from the contact with yours.

Cyril spoke as he did, wantonly, in an hour when reason and conscience had fallen asleep, and vanity was uppermost; but the words brought the temptation they challenged. Tom read his essay in the class next day with a pompous, boastful air, that exceedingly amused his friends. They perceived at once that he was not its author. When they bantered him about it, he readily told its story, repeating, moreover, for their benefit, Cyril's foolish wish.

The consequence was, that the next Friday evening a knot of idle fellows, unprepared with their essays, yet more in jest than in earnest, betook themselves to Cyril's room. "Rivers!" they cried, entering with a great noise of talk and laughter, "behold your fellow-men in trouble! We've come for help!"

"What's wanted?" cried Cyril cheerfullly looking up from his book.

"We want you to write us each a composi tion, as you did Raddon."

Cyril was taken by surprise. His face clouded a little. "One, two, three, four, five!" he said, counting: "five of you that haven't written your essays! What a division ours is! I wonder you ain't ashamed to give it such a reputation for 'flunking.'"

"We are," said Sine readily; "for the honor of the division don't let us go up to old M'Tafor empty-handed! We don't want to disgrace it so."

"Empty-handed!" said Cyril: "that's one thing; but empty-headed is another! I could not help that, you know, if I was to try."

"No: we wouldn't ask it; but won't you write our essays for us? We'll plank you down a dollar apiece if you will. Say, now!"

"You really suppose," said Cyril, "that I can write five original essays, diverse in style and sentiment, for you lazy fellows?"

"Lazy fellows! hear the ingrate!" cried

Benson. " Remember this, Rivers," and, putting on the manner of his teacher, he began to quote some of his words to the class : " ' The advantage of practice in this kind of writing can hardly be estimated. It furnishes a man with a sort of gauge of his acquirements and his command of them. It gives ease of expression, readiness, ingenuity, and clearness in argument, and affords a motive for gaining useful information upon the topics discussed." See, then, what we offer you, thoughtless youth ! One essay is such a benefit, and we give you the chance to write five ! You couldn't be so blind to your own advantage as to refuse ! "

Cyril laughed, and yet his quick, selfish wisdom caught in earnest the idea so jestingly offered. He was silent a moment; and then he said, rather soberly, " Well, fellows, that's not such nonsense after all. I should think it would be a very curious exercise to write six different essays on the same subject, and see how nearly you could suit each one to the man you wrote it for. I'd just like to try it to see what I could do."

" Oh, do ! " cried Benson in delight. " You can do it as easy as fun. What a joke on old M'Tafor ! and what luck for us boys ! "

" But can he really do it ? " asked Baum incredulously. " Five essays on the same subject ! why, I don't believe anybody could ! "

" He isn't like you, you stupid ! " answered Benson : " he can do any thing in the writing line ! "

" Only there's so short a time," said Cyril ; " only between now and to-morrow morning. I don't know that I want to lose my night's sleep for a joke, or an experiment, either."

" But think of the five dollars ! " said Benson : " you said the other day you wanted some money."

" So I do," said Cyril frankly. " To tell the truth, fellows, I've got to have some, or lose half the fun that goes on this winter. So clear out, and I'll see what I can do for you. Only, mind, I don't make any promises ; and, if you don't like what you get, you needn't complain."

" All right," said Benson. " No danger of that ! The luck's too good to be believed ! "

"Write mine first," he turned to say, as they were going out the door. "No, mine first!" cried the others; and then some one began appropriately to sing, —

> "So say we all of us,
> So say we all;"

and to that song they marched away.

Cyril, left alone, smothered uneasy reflections by setting himself to his task. He forgot its unlawfulness, because it interested his fancy, and gave him room to exercise his ingenuity and imitative skill. He found the work not so hard as he had expected. His best ideas were not needed in any of the compositions he was writing now; for the men he wrote for were none of them as well informed or as accustomed to thinking as himself. He took some of the surface thoughts, and put them into such a form of expression as he knew the pretended authors would be likely to make use of; in one case setting them forth abruptly and in disorder; in another, spinning them out with empty and unmeaning phrases; in a third, hanging them over with flaunting flowers of rhetoric, or swelling them into splurgy flights of sounding sentences. The work began to afford him extreme amusement. He smiled to himself, and sometimes laughed aloud, as some expression that was exactly characteristic of the man he was writing for occurred to him. Every paper that he laid by was a triumph of wit and skill that delighted him. He could imagine the applause his clever work would bring him, and the sly mirth among the young men in the class-room, to-morrow, at the tutor's deception, and no less at the expense of the unconscious readers, whose peculiarities he had so happily hit off in those five characteristic essays.

As he finished and folded the last one, the clock in the chapel tower was striking two. He leaned back in his chair, smiling in complacent revery. He thought he had done one of the cleverest things of his whole college course. Nor did the remembrance of the five dollars he was to be paid for his work discontent him. It opened to him fancies of triumphs sweeter than even those among his classmates, — the triumphs of a favorite in gay society. How easily we are satisfied to measure ourselves by the light words of flattery the world will give us! to exaggerate in fancy its delight in our society, and its opinion of our attractiveness and brilliancy! Have you ever seen, dear reader, some poor inmate of a mad-house who fancied himself a monarch, who called his fantastic rags silk and ermine, his tinsel-decked staff a scepter, and his pasteboard tiara a golden crown? who, complacent in his fancied state, smiled down with condescension upon all other men? How little in hours of vanity do we differ from him! Give the mind, so well governed, a little flattery, even a little deserved praise, a manifestation of unusual love, a glimpse of some small success, and straightway we sit down like the madman, and inflate the plain and ordinary circumstances of our lives into airy castles, and enthrone therein ourselves, glorified with wonderful wit, goodness, and beauty, and surrounded with the admiring homage and deep devotion of many lovers and friends. We say to ourselves at such times, "I am more fortunate than other men, better gifted; my judgment is so good, my disposition is so sweet, I win admiration without an effort." When we are tranced in such foolish happiness, with more pity than we look upon the madman, God, who knows in truth how miserable and blind and wanting in all things we are, looks down upon us; and upon such hours, when the humiliation sure to come has opened our eyes, with what scorn and shame do we look back!

Into such an infatuation of vanity, Cyril had fallen, — an infatuation in which men have many times been liars and cheats, and gone about afterward with complacent minds, astonished to hear the world call them reprobates. Cyril was dazzled by looking at his own gifts more than at the fullness of the Giver. He went to bed prayerless that night; for he felt no need of prayer.

CHAPTER VII.

PLEASURE WON, AND HONOR LOST.

"The end of that mirth is heaviness."

TILL under the influence of such a mood as I have described in the last chapter, increased by the success of his essays, and the wonder and amusement of his classmates over them, Cyril went the next evening to see Miss Kerlie. Behold him happily at home in the beautiful drawing-room, ensconced in a luxurious easy-chair by the piano, where the young lady entertains him, now with a little music, and now with lively chat, and all the while with the sight of her pretty dress, and animated, smiling face. She is telling him of her plans for the party, with which she is to open the series that Cyril has promised to attend. It is to be a charade-party ; but she wishes to make it altogether original and brilliant, arranged so as to be as interesting to the audience as to the actors. But she has thought over it so much, and considered so many plans, that she is quite worried and confused, and can not decide which to adopt. She wishes Mr. Rivers would give her the help of his judgment. She is sure he has taste and skill in such matters, and could help her make the affair a perfect success.

Cyril is nothing loth, and they look over the charade-books together. It appears to Cyril that the most satisfactory plays his companion has been able to discover are not as original or as pretty and witty as she could wish them to be. The wish to please her sets his imagination at work; and some bright ideas upon which to get up an evening's entertainment, superior to any of those mentioned in the book, come into his mind. He lays them before her as attractively as he knows how. She is delighted, and casts away her book at once. Mr. Rivers has described exactly what she was in search of. It would be charming. If he can help her get up something of that kind, how much obliged to him she shall be! So, when the evening had been passed in pleasant discussion, Cyril goes away engaged to write Miss Kerlic's charades.

His mind is working over them all the way home: it is full of pretty fancies, and odd and bright conceits. Though it is ten o'clock on Saturday night when he reaches his room, he loses no time in getting pen and paper to give his thoughts shape in words. Midnight comes upon him while he is still absorbed in the work. He lingers over it, and can not bear to put it aside, though the first hours of the Sabbath have arrived. He does not put it out of his mind. He dreams over it; and when he wakes late the next morning, and hurries through his toilet while the prayer-bell is ringing its last peals, his thoughts revert again to the work they hardly left when he fell asleep.

He is languid and tired this morning, and has a feeling, which makes him vexed and peevish, of having but little control over mind or body. His feet stumble upon the stairs; his hands fumble in trying to find the place in the hymn-book; his head and eyes are heavy; and his thoughts, how they will run upon things he should forget at this hour! He can not listen to the Scripture or the prayer. Miss Kerlie's bright parlor, her conversation, her charades, will occupy his imagination in spite of all his efforts, till he almost hates them for haunting him so. It is partly the want of sleep that ails Cyril: he has defrauded himself of rest almost every night this week; and he must pay the penalty mentally and physically. But he suffers no less in temper from having for a while lost the government of his mind in giving himself up to the pleasing delusions of vanity. There is dissipation without the wine-cup, or the gaming-table, or noisy companions. All those fall into it who lose the rule over themselves in any feeling, whether of anxiety, love, covetousness, or self-complacency. Diminishing of strength and scattering of powers are always its sad consequences; and all are liable to them whose lives are not bound steadfastly back to the Giver's, made hourly subject to his laws, and recipients of his grace.

That Sunday was a restless day of discontent to Cyril. No word in the service of the chapel seemed to take hold upon his mind to comfort or please him, or to clear away the vain thoughts that clouded it. At Sunday school he revived a little; for Clara Kerlie was there, and smiled at him from across the room, and the society of scholars and teachers seemed to restore him. But it was only the little taste of favor and flattery that he contrived to extract from their society, that had pleased him again for a while, and it soon left him as unhappy as before.

The week-days that followed, however, brought him enough of what he craved. His charades written out and approved, that was not enough. He must supervise the elaborate arrangements for their getting up, select the actors, and direct the acting, take the chief part himself, and inspire all the others. He found enough to keep him busy with Miss Kerlie and her gay companions every spare moment of the next two weeks. And, when the charades had passed off brilliantly, they proved but the beginning of engagements of the same kind. Cyril was admired and popular: he was beset with invitations to great parties and small; he was asked to assist at theatricals and musicals and dancing soirees; and everywhere he was flattered.

These temptations were of a kind he could not resist: he fell into them recklessly. He lost the fresh ambition he had brought back to college, in a few months of this pleasure-seeking. He declared to himself, that he could, at all events, be a respectable scholar, and that to work so hard and self-denyingly to be a shining one was not worth while. He forgot his father; he forgot the uses of industry that had once seemed so bright even to a selfish view; saddest of all, he forgot his covenant vows, when, in the presence of God, of angels, and the church assembly, he had promised to live soberly, righteously, and godly in this present world, looking for the appearing of the Lord. What a contrast the life described in those words presented to his own!

But there is this comfort in thinking of Cyril,

and of all, who, like him, have gone astray,— God has not forgotten his promises to them, though they have betrayed theirs to him. Night and day, he watches over them, waiting for time to send an awakening voice. Night and day, his hand is upon the circumstances of their lives, using each to do his loving will; till, when his erring children have wandered on as far as to the bitter punishment they have laid up for themselves, he may bring them back in repentance to his feet.

The first complication Cyril found in his career was its cost. He thought he had provided for that when he sold the essays. But he had not calculated for a change in his feelings about expenditure. The sight of elegance begets the wish for it. Constant intercourse with those who spend lavishly tempts to the like carelessness in those whose means are scanty. It was not long before Cyril, coming into a brilliant parlor, and threading his way among the beautiful trails of lace and silk and satin, felt his homely, rusty coat out of place, and kept himself studiously from near contrast with Harry Richman, in his shining dress-suit, laced shirt-front, and diamond studs. There was no help for him in that respect, however; and he could resign himself the better, that the fairest lady of all would rather have his company than Harry's, for all his splendor. But there were little expenses Cyril could not help indulging in : there were the concert tickets he was tempted to buy for the ladies of whose hospitality he had been the recipient; and there was the fair they had got up for some benevolent purpose, that it would have been discourteous, certainly, for him not to invest in. A hundred such ways of spending, that gave his companions not a moment's thought, embarrassed him every day. No wonder he resorted again and again to writing compositions, for which there was always a demand. It took time he could ill spare, and he felt that it was degrading work. But most dangerous of all was the fact, that, relying upon this resource, Cyril grew all the while less self-denying and more extravagant, often exceeding the money in hand, and finding debts more easily made than canceled. In such extremities, it was another misfortune that Tom Raddon was at hand, glad to lend his friend any thing he asked.

When a man's character is lowering ever so slightly, how soon the fact is known among his fellows! If they love him, they do not speak of it; but they know it all the same. Cyril's classmates admired him for his talents, and loved him for his gentle, pleasant disposition. They never blamed him publicly or privately; yet his standing in their respect was not quite as high as it had been last year. His acts were, of course, patent among them. It was well known by most of them that he wrote compositions for sale, that he was in Raddon's debt, and that he was more occupied with gay society than was right for a man in his position. Though they never censured him, they knew he was doing wrong. So instinctively were they silent concerning his actions among those who would be shocked by them, that John Seelye, very much occupied in his own pursuits, had never yet heard of the things of which I have been telling you.

But, one Friday evening, Seelye and Stavins were passing Cyril's room on their way to the prayer-meeting. "I wonder," said John, looking up at the light in the windows, "if Rivers would not go with us to-night."

"It's Friday night," said Stavins. "I am afraid he'll be busy writing the fellows' essays."

"The fellows' essays!" said John surprised. "What do you mean?"

"Oh!" said Nollie, "I thought you knew. I forgot. Never mind about it."

"But what do you mean?" persisted John.

"Why," said Nollie, "you see the fellows get belated with their compositions, and they pay him to write them for them, he writes so easily. I wish he wouldn't do it; but none of them seem to think it's any harm."

"Are you sure he does that? Do you know positively?" asked John. He spoke with so severe a tone, that Nollie, frightened for Cyril, tried his best to say truthfully something that might exculpate him.

"I never saw him do it," he said, "nor talked about it with any of the fellows he did it for. But it is the common story. I have got used to hearing it : I thought you had. I should not have spoken of it."

"No, you should not," said John earnestly. "There can't be any truth in it. No man could do such a thing who was not lost to shame. I could hardly believe it of Rivers if I heard it from his own lips. It's gossip, got up because of his patience with Raddon and that childish set. They hang round him as the poor boys do in our mission school. He has got some strange gift for pleasing and influencing them. Don't tell me, that, instead of trying to do them good, he would lend himself to ruining them. I will not believe it."

John was much agitated. His thoughts had flown to the mission school, to Cyril's work there, to his influence, his speeches, his prayers. Could it be that this man John had thought likely to be so useful was false? John loved the school; and the bare suspicion filled him with jealousy for its welfare. Well it might; for, though the story were proved to be slanderous, its very existence was prejudicial to Cyril.

It could not have gained credence for a moment about a thoroughly true man like John.

Nollie Stavins knew in his heart that the story was true; but he was willing enough to let John disbelieve it. No more was said between them upon the subject.

But every Sabbath after that it seemed to Cyril, that, in chapel or Sunday school, he never raised his eyes from his class or book, but he met the troubled glance of John Seelye fixed upon him. He met it at first carelessly, then with wonder, and then with dread, and, at last, learned to avoid meeting it; a consciousness of shame and unworthiness, every time that he did so, coming like a cloud over the bright atmosphere of worldly favor in which he had wrapped himself.

A little incident that occurred about this time served to increase the uneasiness he felt in thinking of John Seelye. In one of the teachers' meetings occurred the annual election of officers for the school; and Cyril was nominated for secretary and treasurer. Of course, as it was an office of small responsibility, which any one of average intelligence and faithfulness could hold, and as Cyril was so popular, there was no expectation of any thing but a unanimous vote in his favor. There was a slight sensation of surprise, then, when the superintendent counted one adverse vote. No one noticed it much, however, except Cyril. Instinctively, he glanced across the room at John Seelye. There was a shade of some sad feeling softening his face; but he met Cyril's gaze quietly. Nevertheless, Cyril was sure that John had cast that vote.

Cyril went home that night with a sorrow in his heart almost as bitter as if the whole world had distrusted and rejected him, instead of one man. Perhaps it was because he had such reason, in his real unworthiness, to dread the first sign of distrust.

Shall we inquire what had actuated John? Suppose he had good reason to believe Cyril careless of honesty about his every-day work; even then, could it be feared he would betray the little trust they proposed to give him in the school? The thing would be impossible.

There were bonds enough to secure him in this case, of course.   He would not risk losing his character as a gentleman, and being held up to the reprobation of the community, for any such trivial temptation.

But John could not reason in that way.   To him, the man who did not live the truth in the fear of God was never reliable ; no, not when backed by the strongest securities, and by the strongest motives of worldly wisdom.   Such a man he could not help place in any trust, however slight, especially a trust in the service of God.   And in John's little action I think there was a good lesson in political management for Tom Raddon to learn.   If a man is unfaithful to his own best interests, do not put those of others into his hands in the blind hope that he will deal with them more justly and wisely.

CHAPTER VIII.

TOM AND HIS TEACHER.

"The borrower is servant to the lender."

OWARD the close of the winter, one rainy Saturday afternoon, Tom Raddon was walking up and down Cyril's room, suffering from " nothing to do." That simply meant that he did not want to work, and could think of no pleasure that attracted him. He was in a very discontented frame of mind, and was pouring forth a long catalogue of complaints to patient Cyril. He cursed the weather, he found fault with his friends, he detailed his misfortunes,— the letter of warning sent home to his father, his father's displeasure in consequence, his own folly of heart and stupidity of head, his disappointment in the make of his new suit, and his vexation because his boots were too large,—

and expressed in general his conviction that there was nothing in life worth living for, and that he would about as lief be a poor dog as a man. Now, of all selfishness, the most wanton is laying the burden of one's petty griefs and vexations upon a friend in fretful complaint. Cyril, at this dreary close of the week, was enough depressed with troubles of his own; but he listened to Tom with great gentleness and patience, sympathizing with him, or trying to reason with him, or laugh away his vagaries. If he had not himself forgotten what can keep a man always strong and joyful, he might have given Tom something better than this kind endurance of his fretfulness; that is, a few faithful words to have shown its cause and its prevention.

From other troubles, Tom at last proceeded to descant upon his pecuniary vexations. He had lost money at play; all the bills that had been sent in to him had proved twice as large as he had expected, and there were some he did not believe he had ever made, — he had no recollection whatever of having done so. His father had utterly refused to increase again his stipulated quarterly allowance, which, large as it was, he had exceeded every quarter since he had been in college, and this time more carelessly than ever. There was no hope of inducing him to change his decision since that letter had gone home. It had made him very angry. Tom could not tell what to do: he had never been so " hard up " in his life.

Now, when he came to this part of his grumbling, Cyril dropped the pencil with which he had been idly sketching upon the leaf of a book, and instead of the weary look upon his face came one of shame and distress. Borrowing from Tom had been such an easy matter, that it had been repeated till the amount which Cyril owed him was considerable. Tom had forgotten it, or he would not have complained of his poverty in his friend's hearing: there was enough delicacy in him for that; but, since he did complain, Cyril remembered the debt, and was ashamed.

" I wish I could pay you the money you lent me, Tom," he said at last. " I have not for-

gotten it: but my father is like yours in thinking I spend too much already; and, unlike
yours, he could not give me more if he would.
It is not his debt, either: it is mine. But I am
afraid you'll have to wait a good while before
I earn the money to pay it."

Tom stopped in his walk, and turned upon
Cyril, his face red with mortification and anger.
"You speak of that again if you dare!" he
said quite savagely. "The sooner you forget
it the better, — as if it was of any account in
the world! Why, there's fellows I do not
care a straw for borrowed and begged of me
more than you can guess, that never dream of
paying up. They just hang round to see how
much sport they can get me to pay for. They
never did any thing for me, as you have done,
and as you can do again too."

Tom's selfishness would assert itself in the
midst of generous and friendly impulses. He
was thinking of something he had had in mind
all day, and had been only waiting an oppor-
tune moment to broach to Cyril. He said
the last words mysteriously, and, stopping in

his walk, drew a chair to the table opposite Cyril.

" What is it ? " said Cyril anxiously.

" Why, it's this," said Tom. " If you can do for me what nobody else can, and what would be worth to me two or three hundred dollars, you'd stop fidgeting about that money, wouldn't you ? "

" Perhaps so," said Cyril. " What is it ? "

" Something I *must* do. It's the only way to please father that I can think of; but, if I should succeed, I should fairly revel in ' dosh ' all next summer."

" Well, speak out," said Cyril impatiently: " what are you thinking of ? "

" Of the prize-debates," said Tom. " I'm going to go in and win one of the prizes. If you'll help me, instead of owing me any thing, I'll be bound to you for ever. If I should succeed, it would be just the thing to make my father think I was getting on at speech-making, and it would set me up in his good graces for a year. Will you show me how to win, Rivers ? "

Cyril looked discouraged. " I can't," he said : " the thing would be impossible, utterly impossible."

" I don't see why," said Tom sulkily, " if you were willing."

" Why, the best writers in the class are going into these debates : how could I make you able to compete with them? And I tell you it would be another thing for me to write your debate for you than to write your composition, especially if it's to be a winning one."

" I don't see why," said Tom again.

" Because, for you to go and compete with somebody else's debate would be altogether too daring a thing. False goods won't bear so strong a light as that. Why, the very fact of your joining in the debate at all, when you are one of the poorest writers in the class, would be surprising ; and if you should bring an essay that compared respectably with the rest, — why, these are not the days of miracles, and everybody would know there was something wrong. Besides, this is different from the compositions, because it's a strife among the fellows, and it would be mean not to go in fairly."

"Hang the fellows!" growled Tom much discomfited, but still holding to his plan with a strong will. "But I tell you, Rivers, I didn't want you to write the debate for me: I asked you to show me how to do it myself. Suppose I am stupid, and suppose I never did write any thing decent in my life, is that any reason why I can't try when I've a mind to? I tell you " — looking at Cyril with a scowl of determination — "I *can* do things when I - please. I've found that out once or twice; and I'd like to try this time. There's a strong enough motive, and I feel it in me that I'll carry my point in some way."

In some way! But could he possibly do it in a fair way? Cyril sighed as the doubtful question passed through his mind.

"Well, of course, you've a right to try," he said; "and it will be a good thing for you. But how can I help you?"

"Why, you know best, I reckon," said Tom. "Tell me how to set to work, in the first place."

"Well, in the first place," said Cyril, "you

want to read up on both sides of the question."

" And what shall I read ? " asked Tom.

Now, Cyril was going to compete for the prize himself, and was, for many reasons, very anxious to win. He had made out a list of books for examination, which, to let Tom use, would be a serious drawback to him, in preventing him from obtaining the volumes when he wanted them, to say nothing of the danger that the material of their essays might be similar, and so the effect and freshness of each be lessened. Yet, after a moment's hesitation, he gave him his list, and explained to him just the plan in using it he followed himself. He told Tom how he must take notes of what he thought most likely to serve his purpose ; how he was to combine the force of arguments found in different places ; how to select the most impressive proofs, and to glean relevant facts to help build up his theory. He told him how he must let his mind work upon what it had gathered, and bestow upon it fresh color and form ; how to set the main points in **due** order in a brief preparatory plan, and then how to fill out the structure upon the frame-work. When Tom grew bewildered and despairing on account of the strangeness and difficulty of the work thus described to him, Cyril would go over the process again, stating it so that it seemed less formidable to him. Cyril understood the lesson and the scholar, and Tom forced himself to attention: so that, at last, he could say that he believed he saw his way clear in beginning the undertaking. There was nothing Cyril told him that books and instructors had not many times tried to teach him; but he had never before had the will to learn.

But Cyril's labor for Tom was only begun. That very evening, he came to Cyril's room again, bringing with him some of the books recommended. There was a scowl upon his face as he flung them upon the table.

"I've been up in my room with these," he said, "ever since supper; but I don't see any use in them. I can't find any thing to the point; or, if there is, I'm too stupid to understand it. You'll have to help me, Rivers: I must make headway somehow."

Cyril had on his overcoat, and was about to go to the teachers' meeting. "I'm going out, Tom," he said: "you'll have to wait till toward nine o'clock, when I come back."

"Oh, dear!" groaned Tom: "I shall be sleepy enough by that time, if I sit here over these heavy books to wait for you. Can't you stay?" His selfishness was so habitual, he was often surprisingly exacting and imperious in his requests.

Cyril considered: it was stormy, and the meeting would be small and uninteresting. True, there would then be more need of his presence and assistance; but that thought did not have much weight with him. And, in the midst of his reflections, there came to his memory the glance of a pair of honest gray eyes, that he did not like to meet, and from the consciousness of which, to-night, in such a small meeting, there would be less to distract him. That half-recognized thought decided him. He threw off his coat.

"I won't go," said he. "I'd rather stay and read. You see I can do my work helping you. I can kill two birds with one stone. I thought I should have to wait for these books till you got through with them; but now we'll read on together, and I shall get the gist of the matter more surely myself by pointing it out to you."

Tom was touched by his readiness to oblige, and thanked him with a look of gratitude. "Rivers," he said, as they drew their chairs to the table, "what are you going to do when you get through college?"

" Why, I haven't made up my mind," said Cyril. "If I should get an opportunity, I might stay here as tutor, and some day work up to be a learned professor."

Tom stared at him incredulously. " You wouldn't?" said he.

" Why, yes," said Cyril. "It's a kind of life I used to think might be pleasant. But perhaps I shall be a lawyer: I've thought more of that lately, because, you see, it pays better."

"Do," said Tom, apparently much relieved, "and come down to San Francisco to open your office. My father can help you to business. He'll make a rich man of you before you're thirty."

"And then," said Cyril, smiling, "I can take you for a partner, and help you into Congress, just as I'm going to help you win this prize."

Tom shook his head. "You couldn't," said he ruefully. "Every tub'll have to stand on its own bottom after a while. A man can't be helped always."

True enough, Tom; truer than you perceive. No one can long stand between you and the results of your indolence. Cyril, from motives partly selfish, partly amiable, helps you now; but you must stand for yourself at the examination: you must answer for yourself to your father when you go back without the knowledge he sent you to obtain; for yourself to the world, which expects a return from your manhood for all of pleasure and teaching it has bestowed upon your youth; for yourself to your God, when he finds you, after shower and sunshine, after many golden seasons of opportunity, still only a useless cumberer of the ground. And you, Cyril, who have been so trained in the consideration of truths like these, that, even now, they troop dimly, like unnoticed shadows, through your mind, why will you not stop, and kindly point them out to your friend, while he is for a moment pausing, and looking with alarmed eyes into the future?

Before they began to read, Cyril talked over the subject a little, giving Tom such an idea of it as he himself already possessed. When they opened the books, Cyril was, nevertheless, obliged often to point out how the reading was connected with the subject, and threw light upon it; or he stopped frequently to bid Tom take notes, or to ask his thoughts, or to express his own. In this way, as Tom earnestly gave his attention, his interest was soon aroused, and his mind set at work. He began readily to exchange his roughly expressed but fresh and original ideas with Cyril's. It became evident to the latter that Tom would voluntarily take the opposite side of the debate from the one he had chosen to advocate; and that he thought very fortunate. This interchange of ideas he found was not unprofitable ; for, though Tom's line of thought was narrower, and more likely to be erring, than Cyril's, yet Cyril found his mind quickened and enlightened by exploring it. And Tom, in trying to argue with Cyril, and in hearing him talk, began to be delighted with the new wisdom he seemed himself to have gained, and the profundity of thought he had found in himself. It was as if a whole new field of knowledge lay at his command, which he was the more proud of, because part of it, at least, was gained by his own discovery. He went home almost as triumphant of heart as though he already carried the prize in his pocket.

Imagine Cyril's astonishment, when, three days after this, Tom came in and announced his essay as finished.

"So soon!" said Cyril. "Why, I expect to be over mine the whole of the next three weeks."

“ Very likely,” said Tom. “ But I can’t do that. It’s ‘ strike while the iron is hot ’ with me. I know I’ve done it better than if I’d bored over it longer. Here, I’ve brought it for you to read. I’ll venture to say there won’t be but one better, — yours, of course. There’s some fire in this, I guess, that’ll carry the judges by storm. It’s got what *I think* in it, spoken out pretty plain. I mean to send it to my father : it ought to please him, if nothing else will.”

Cyril, not much re-assured by Tom’s perfect satisfaction with his work, sat down to read it. It was written in Tom’s most dashing hand, and made quite a bulky manuscript. But, alas! its formidable appearance did not make up for the failure of its contents. Its commencement was abrupt and awkward, its statements pompous and puerile and unsustained, its arguments obscure, its illustrations absurd, its style of the spread-eagle variety, deforming and concealing whatever there really existed in the thought that was true and forcible. Moreover, Tom had omitted entirely many of the most important points of the discussion, and had committed the egregious blunder of mentioning opposing arguments, without attempting to refute them. The essay had every possible fault. Cyril read it, as much perplexed as amused. He could not tell what to say as he finished it, and looked up to meet Tom's confident gaze.

"Well," said Tom, "isn't that about the thing?"

Cyril hesitated, finding it hard to answer. At last he said, "No, old fellow: you're not out of the woods yet, by any means. You mustn't be in such a hurry. You've got to go over this three or four times before you will be done."

"Why, what's the matter with it?" asked Tom, his face falling.

"Oh! a good many things," said Cyril. "But, before we go any farther, Tom, do let me ask you what's the use of your doing this any way? I wish you'd give it up."

"Why, I told you what I was doing it for," said Tom; "and I will not give it up."

" But I don't believe it's necessary, Tom. I can show you how to write such a letter to your father as will bring you all the money you want."

" I tell you you don't know any thing about my father," answered Tom. " He isn't to be moved by any ' bosh.' He's a hard man, and used to dealing with facts. He always looks out to get the worth of his money, seeing he made it himself; and, if I don't *do* something to prove to him that it isn't money wasted to keep me here, nothing else will satisfy him. So tell me what I've got to do to this thing," taking up the essay. " I've half a mind to speak it exactly as it is."

" To tell the truth, Tom," said Cyril, " I don't believe they'll let you go on to the stage with it."

He persuaded Tom to sit down, and patiently pointed out the most glaring errors, showed him that he was not yet half acquainted with his subject, and that his statement of what he did know was disorderly and incomplete. For two or three days more, they worked together over the essay, till Cyril, pressed by his own occupations, and driven to despair by his pupil's incompetency, did what he knew was wrong. Cyril knew how the subject ought to be handled ; but, finding he could not make Tom conform to his ideas in any other way, he dictated to him, word for word, a complete abstract of what he thought the essay ought to be, setting every point and argument and proof in its order, omitting nothing. He persuaded himself that this was no worse than any other way of helping Tom ; that to write out for him those few hints need not prevent him from calling the work his own. Then he explained to him how to work out every point, and earnestly endeavored to persuade him to adopt a simpler style than the bombastic one of the stump-orator.

After all this, Tom, whose determination never flagged through much hard work and discouragement, and whose patience and docility had amazed Cyril, once more brought him his finished essay. It was incomparably better than the first ; but this time he presented it with as much doubt as he had shown confidence before. Cyril sighed to see how much more work was still to be done. The essay showed its beautiful framework still half covered. It was like a house of noble plan, but all unfinished, — the clapboarding nailed on only in places, the windows unglazed, the paint put on in patches, and of different colors, and the steps for approach still wanting. Alas! it was strange to see how much more faithful was Cyril to his notion of perfection in the piece than to truth and fairness in helping Tom write it.

Once more, the two sat down together; and Cyril passed in review every word of the essay, altering, and introducing whole sentences and paragraphs, pruning out what was redundant, simplifying what was overstrained, and correcting what was false and ungrammatical. You might think the essay itself would have testified against them; but Cyril proceeded very artfully. He purposely left some roughness and abruptness, and whatever he could that was characteristic of Tom: so that there was nothing in the composition but its general ability and completeness to prove it a fraud.

Cyril sighed with relief when he at length saw the work finished, yet he trembled at its excellence. Tom felt no such satisfaction in it as he had done in the first efforts he had made all by himself, though he would still have declared himself ready to affirm upon his honor that the essay was his own. The reality of its authorship, let them deceive themselves as they might, was plainly enough proved to them by the fact, that, while Tom found great difficulty in committing his essay to memory, Cyril already knew every word of it by heart.

The fact, too, that, by this time, the very subject of the debate had become unpleasant to him might have told Cyril something. He hated to commence writing upon his own essay. In spite of his father's and classmates' expectations, and his own desire to win a prize, he would have withdrawn from the contest if a secret dread had not suggested to him, that his being a competitor would avert suspicion from him in case Tom's debate was received with doubt. Driven by this thought, he sat himself to work laboriously. Besides all he had already thought upon the subject, he sought new sources of information, and soon found himself gaining new ideas and a deeper insight into the matter. His interest and ambition were roused again; and, as his prospect of success grew every day more certain, he forgot the uneasiness that the work he had done for Tom had left upon his mind. In vanity and self-confidence he hardened himself against his guilt, so that he soon became almost unconscious that it was guilt.

CHAPTER IX.

TOM'S SUCCESS.

"Excellent speech becometh not a fool ; much less do lying lips a prince."

OM'S name upon the list of competitors for the prize debates surprised Professor M'Tafor. Tom had shirked his compositions with such boldness and persistency, that his undertaking a voluntary labor of the kind, when he was so unprepared for it, was truly astonishing. His essay, when it was handed in with the others for criticism, completed the good man's amazement. At first, he was pleased; and then, upon further consideration, a painful suspicion took possession of him: so that, at last, he summoned Tom to a conference.

Although Tom and Cyril had never allowed to each other or themselves that they were acting unfairly, yet that summons filled them both with consternation. Tom, however, after a few moments' hesitation, and trembling of heart, professed himself ready to brave the matter out. He had made up his mind, he said, that the thing should be carried through successfully; and it should not fail for want of "brass" on his part. He had nothing to be afraid of, and he had as lief meet Professor M'Tafor as any other man. With that he buttoned up his double-breasted coat, as a man might buckle his armor, and made his appearance before the professor, his rough face wearing its boldest and most dogged scowl.

Mr. M'Tafor was a gentle, kind-hearted man. The soul of honor himself, it was only from sad experience with his charge, that he had learned to suspect the prevalence of falsehood among others. It was unpleasant to him to express to Tom the doubt upon which he had sent for him; but he knew the best way in hard tasks is to proceed to them directly, even if it must be bluntly.

"Mr. Raddon," he said, "I have been surprised at the great difference between your debate and every thing of the kind you have before produced. It was so great, that I must ask an explanation of it."

"Sir," said Tom, his countenance, as he said it should be, like "brass," "it's very easily explained. I care nothing about our weekly compositions; but, for the strongest possible reason, I wanted to win one of those prizes. I wrote with the determination to win one."

The professor studied Tom's hard face, much perplexed. "But I have never seen in you, Mr. Raddon, any proof whatever of the ability to write such an essay as this, even with the most urgent motives."

"Well, sir," answered Tom, doggedly holding his ground, "I never had the ability before: I worked up to it with harder work than I ever had in all my life, just for this."

There was a short pause, during which the professor seemed puzzled how to proceed. At last he said, —

"Mr. Raddon, it is my duty to speak plainly with you. Notwithstanding what you have said, I can scarcely believe this essay is your own entirely unassisted work. But I have no proof of this, and can not, by my misgivings, keep you out of the lists. But I ask you, by your honor as a gentleman, if you know of any reason why you can not with perfect fairness to your companions, and with truth and credit to yourself, bring this essay into competition, to withdraw it now."

" I shall not withdraw it," said Tom : " it is my own." There was a bad look upon his face, a glance of the unscrupulous fierceness with which his will trampled down some tender impulses to good that moved in his heart. The professor saw that look with uneasiness, though he tried to suppose it only an expression of the anger a man might naturally feel at being unjustly suspected. At any rate, he felt himself bound to believe so after Tom's answer. He held out his hand, saying kindly, —

" Then forgive my suspicions. I am, of course, quite satisfied with that assurance. Only let me hope you will not suffer the use of such powers as you here display to cease with the motive which led to their discovery."

Tom departed, his face still scowling, his manner of flinging out of the room still apparently indicating outraged honesty. But there was a feeling in his heart that dismayed him, a terror about what he was doing, a sense of misery and shame, that made him nearly desperate. He stalked up and down under the elms, his bad resolution not in the least shaken, but his mind in a passion of discontent. He was angry with Cyril as well as himself. He asked why Cyril had given him undue help, or why he was not as much shocked, if the thing was so wrong, as the professor would have been if he had known all. It was too late now: if the thing was mean, Tom said, he could not help it. He did not wish to defraud the other fellows; but, if any of 'em had worked harder than he, let 'em prove it. He must have that prize: he had not so set his mind upon any thing in his whole college course. The rest might take the other honors: he had never asked for any but this. If there was any thing wrong in the way he was competing, had he not done enough for the class to be excused, —

he who had bought the boat, and spent so much money in other ways for class purposes?

Thus he tried to reason away his remorse. But all that day, and for many succeeding ones, his manner was almost savage, and his face fiercely scowling. His companions wondered to see him so very irritable. They attributed his mood to the trouble he had spoken of between himself and his father. There was considerable amusement at the report that he was to be one of the speakers; but when one of his familiar comrades jokingly congratulated him upon his new ambition, Tom cut him short so angrily, and was always so cross when the debates were mentioned, that his friends hardly dared speak of them in his presence.

Well, the day for the speaking came at last, and brought some unexpected results. The judges were persons not in any way connected with the college, and likely to be entirely impartial. Cyril carried away the first prize. His speech was conspicuously the best in thought, expression, and delivery. The second was won by a scholar with whom we are not acquainted ; and the third was divided between Tom Raddon and John Seelye.

Those who knew these two had listened to them with surprise. John had never been very fortunate as a writer; but, by much pains-taking, he had this once, at least, contrived to express some true and original thoughts in plain, clear language, very forcibly. His un-usual success, however, no one thought of con-sidering as any thing but the result of honest, industrious effort. His speech was heard with no such wonder and incredulity as Tom's first sentences began to excite among those ac-quainted with his former attainments.

Tom was unnaturally excited, as those knew who were most familiar with him, — those who had laughed slyly to see him run out to a neighboring bar-room for a glass of brandy just before his turn to speak. It was by fair means or foul, by true fire or false, that he was bound to compel success. When he stood upon the platform, those physical advantages upon which his ignorant father had calculated did really tell in his favor. His tall and powerful figure, his large head, and heavy, strongly-marked features, were impressive. The scowl upon his forehead made him look terribly in earnest. His cheeks burned, and there was fire in his dark eyes. Altogether, he appeared like a man of force and ability; and Cyril, trembling with anxiety, was relieved, as he looked at Tom, to see that the well-known words of that essay would not appear incongruously wise from his lips. He began to speak well, a little too forcibly for Cyril's taste perhaps; but the fault might have served him with many not so fastidious. Cyril's anxiety for him was so extreme, that his own lips actually moved in unison with Tom's throughout the piece. It was fortunate for both, that the wonder with which those near were listening to the speaker prevented them from noticing this little circumstance.

Whatever surprise and half-suspicion the excellence of Tom's essay had at first excited in some minds, it was so good, and he delivered it with such effect, that classmates as well as strangers joined in the round of applause that greeted him when he finished. That applause, the token of his success, was the first thing that dispelled the remorse that had been vexing Tom's soul these many days. He looked about, the frown upon his forehead disappearing in a triumphant smile; and there was a touch of his own old braggart, self-satisfied manner in the bow of thanks he returned, as he stalked off the stage, that afforded his friends infinite amusement.

The judges, with one exception, agreed to rank Tom third. But one of them had been pleased with John Seelye's speech. He had listened to it very attentively, and thought it showed peculiar merit. He recalled it to the minds of the others, and argued its claims so well, that he secured the agreement of his associates to let it share the third prize.

This arrangement was of little consequence to Tom. The name of having taken a prize was all he cared for. That he could now send to San Francisco the college journal containing an account of the debate, with the complimentary notice of his essay, and the announcement that he had ranked third among twenty contestants, was enough to serve his purpose. In his delight, he invited all the debaters, together with his intimate friends, to a supper in honor of his success, and was congratulated by them all in apparent good faith. Those who could not help holding suspicions held them privately. No one wanted to make an unpleasant disturbance. The general feeling was, that Tom was a " good fellow," and had always shown a great deal of class liberality; and, if he had a strong desire to carry his point this once, there was no use in seeking to thwart him.

Cyril, when he saw matters terminating thus favorably, took heart again also. He forgot all that he had suffered about the fraud, — forgot, almost, that he had committed it. His own success was no light thing to him. He was complimented upon it at every turn. His father was pleased; and he had his twenty-dollars prize in his pocket. He forgot the anxieties that had made him rather more industrious of late, and gave way more carelessly than ever to vanity and pleasure-seeking. Having made proof to his ambition of his superior ability, he thought he could now rest upon his oars a while; that his honor would shine bright enough without his care.

He went through the rest of the year half working, and was not nearly as much chagrined, at its close, to discover his loss in standing as he had been the year before. He took home, to satisfy his father, a philosophic coolness about his failure, an assertion that he had been learning more from life, if less from books, and that to bury himself in his studies would be to miss sympathy with his fellows, and knowledge of human nature, and to grow selfish in a narrow and mean ambition. To which his father gravely answered, that to be diligent in business hindered no man from being fervent in spirit; and that the student whose single aim was to serve the Lord, serving himself and others in the truest way, by consequence, could neither be a poor scholar, nor a selfish, narrow-minded man.

As for Tom, he was not disappointed in the

effect of his prize and the reading of his essay upon his father. In all the course of his hard life, the old man had met no greater gratification than this promise of his son's future success. He went about, the proudest man in San Francisco. As if to make up for having wronged Tom in his dissatisfaction, he sent him a large sum of money, with the liberty to draw for whatever more he needed. Like Cyril, Tom, upon the strength of his success, gave himself up to idleness and extravagance, till the closing examination of the year drew nigh. Then, finding there was great likelihood of being dropped to the class below, he fell to making desperate exertions. Day and night, for three weeks, he and Baum, whose delinquencies were like his own, shut themselves up together "to cram." With any number of translations and keys, they found it a difficult matter to do a year's work in less than a month. They pasted together strips of paper to the length of several feet, and copied nearly a whole book of mathematical formulas upon them. These strips were attached to little rollers, one at either end, which rolled up to meet each other. As, fast, then, as by the motion of the fingers, the paper was coiled over one roller, it was drawn from the other; so that the whole surface could in a few moments be passed under review, hidden in one's hand. By the help of this contrivance, and many other ingenious and painstaking methods of cheating, but much more by the help of what real study they were able to accomplish, they contrived to scramble through the examination; and with that they were abundantly satisfied.

CHAPTER X.

THE PROMENADE CONCERT.

" Open rebuke is better than secret love."

I PASS on to the third winter of Cyril's life at college. Of what was unfortunate in his course, one thing he would have been ready to confess, — he was not growing happier. The failures in scholarship, that he professed to look upon with such indifference, were secretly galling to him, and took away from his self-respect. He still ran eagerly after social pleasures ; but they never now proved so delightful as formerly. He was developing slightly the saddest of all symptoms in a young man, — professed disgust with what life offers. He cheapened its best gifts to his mind, because he did not want to make the effort to win them ; and low and easy pleasures were palling upon his taste. His friendships were often a vexation to him, because he had not founded them upon truth. Of himself he was fast losing expectation. He was beginning to persuade himself that no man was good, unselfish, or honest, no pleasure satisfactory, no hope worth aiming for. This perverse and infidel reasoning always ensues in minds, that, with a naturally quick perception of the right, yield to sin. They must blind and harden themselves to escape torture from violated instincts. But such a false view of life and manhood is deadly: it is the paralytic stroke which the Devil deals to kill energy and fervor of spirit, and to put an end to the last feeble struggles of the soul after its true nobility. True, there is an existence which merits such a contemptuous estimate: it is that which is alienated from the life of God. Well may those who have separated from him deem that there is no joy or fullness or profit in their lives, and call them mean and worthless. But let them not offend God by saying that the gifts of the being he gave them were such. It is they who with

their own hands have plucked out its priceless
jewels, and thrown them away, — the jewels of
possible wisdom and joy and holiness and
immortality, drawn from the treasures of Him
who filleth all in all.

But, beside his secret dissatisfaction with
himself, Cyril had other causes of sorrow, which
it was less in his power to remove. A cloud
hung over his home, arising from the growing
feebleness of Mr. Rivers's health, at a time
when the wants of his family and congregation
were making greater demands than ever before
upon his exertions. Cyril, in the last weeks
of his vacation, could not help noticing how his
father's figure stooped from weakness, how
often he sighed over his work, and how easily
he grew tired. He could not help seeing the
extreme anxiety of his mother and older sisters
about his father's health, and hearing their
perplexed consultations as to how to relieve
him of the burdens that his shoulders seemed
the only ones to bear. Cyril had once proposed leaving college as the best means for sav-
ing expense : but they told him that was not to

be thought of; that his father could bear any thing better than such a disappointment. So he had come back to college, anxious at heart whenever he thought of home troubles. But, to some extent, he forgot them as the weeks separated him from what he had seen of them, and the cheerful letters he received defended him from the knowledge of their continuance, and as he became more and more absorbed in himself, and his present circumstances and occupations.

Who projected the grand promenade concert in aid of the Orphan Asylum, with anticipations of which the town was now full? No doubt the scheme was got up between the fertile wits of little Miss Kerlie — whose benevolent concern for mission schools and orphans was always uniting itself with her passion for social excitement — and those of her old bachelor *confrère*, Mr. Rollin Childs, that invaluable man in society, of liberal fortune and infinite good nature, whose whole occupation and end in life seemed to be to help with his means and his energies the sports of the young ladies.

They laughed at him for the frivolity they encouraged, not reflecting that it was no more unbecoming — though, let us hope, more unusual — in a man of middle life than in women, who, if some of them were his juniors, were at least of adult intelligence and powers, and as capable of an earnest purpose in living as he.

Well, the Orphan Asylum was in want of funds, and Miss Kerlie and Mr. Childs were in want of pleasing occupation. Therefore, it was one morning reported in the daily paper of Eaton, that " some enterprising and wealthy young gentlemen of our city had a plan on foot for relieving one of our most deserving and popular charities, the Orphan Asylum. The scheme proposed was one likely to be eminently successful, if carried out as the names of those who had it in charge guaranteed that it would be carried out, and must be gratifying in itself, aside from its praiseworthy object, to all lovers of good taste and the most refined social pleasures." Then followed an account of what had been planned. The concert was to be made a most select and elegant affair; the tickets were to sell at five dollars each, and the entire expenses to be defrayed, if possible, by subscription : so that the profits might be clear. A second meeting of those interested had been appointed ; and all who were willing to co-operate were earnestly desired to attend.

Cyril, turning over the paper in the college reading-room, saw this promising notice, but paid little attention to it. But he afterward became more interested, when he discovered with what enthusiasm Miss Kerlie and the large circle of her friends had entered into the plan. They could talk of nothing else. The concert, as they declared, was to be the most elegant, delightful, and brilliant affair the city had ever known, and to be an immense help to the asylum. Moreover, Cyril was not left to suppose that it was a town affair, and he had nothing to do with it. It was exceedingly important that the students should be induced to co-operate. Their attendance at the concert would be indispensable, and their help was much desired in preparing for it. Cyril, if he would, could do a great deal to help enlist them in the cause. He must invite them to attend the next meeting of the Aid Association, and go himself.

Cyril felt little inclination to accept these hints. He felt that he should be quite out of place at such a meeting, having nothing to subscribe ; and he dreaded that some entanglement might result. But when he reported what he had heard to Benson and Sine and others, who, not having as slender a purse as his own, eagerly hailed the prospect of a new pleasure, their interest awakened his. They were ready enough to attend the meeting, and see how the preparations were progressing ; and Cyril agreed to accompany them.

The projectors of the plan were very glad to receive them, and to press into the service their energy and ingenuity. Therefore, when the various officers and committees of the new Aid Association had been appointed, while the wealthy and *solid* men of the city had their names, with or without their consent, placed in a long list as vice-presidents, and members of the finance committee, to insure the monetary success of the affair, Cyril Rivers and several more of his college friends were put down as decorative committee and floor-managers, to guarantee its success as a brilliant entertainment. Mr. Rollin Childs had not studied the management of social gayeties so long for nothing: he had managed it very skillfully.

Cyril was at first vexed and uneasy at the position into which he found himself thrust. But there were some considerations that finally reconciled him to the responsibility. He should, of course, wish to attend the concert; and if he made himself really efficient in getting it up, as very few named for the committees would do, no doubt his services would excuse the purchase of a ticket: then he saw a prospect of some exciting pleasure in the work. No expense was to be spared to render the hall elegant, and Cyril might have full scope to exercise his ingenious and cultivated taste; and then he reflected, with complacency, that, with his handsome person and pleasing manners, he was just the one to win glory on such an occasion in the conspicuous place of a floor-manager. Are you astonished that he should be influenced by such a childish thought? But vanity is so debasing : it is a long and silly madness, if anger is a short and fierce one. Let it overcome a man, and he will not remember any more the pure and high ambition he cherished before. Cyril could sacrifice higher interests to these petty triumphs, and forgot the scorn with which he would have condemned in another the reputation he was himself seeking.

Once having engaged himself in forwarding the concert, Cyril gave himself up to the work with eager interest. He was made chairman of the decorative committee, and took the management of its duties all into his own hands. The design, execution, and oversight were his ; and, the farther he progressed in his work, the more enthusiastic he grew. His plans were extensive and extravagant ; but, as fast as they became evident, they were applauded for their elegance and originality. He enlisted all the help he was able, and got together meetings of his classmates, and of all the young people of the city, to tie evergreens in the hall. He was the inspiration of all the gayety that went on there, as well as commander-in-chief of the activity; and he enjoyed the position. When the remembrance of duties and home anxieties vexed him, he pushed them off till after the concert. That was the one interest that excluded others from his mind at present. He was no worse in this than many others. In fact, a sort of madness about this grand concert, sanctified by its benevolent purpose, seemed to seize upon all the town's people. A great amount of money was contributed toward defraying the expenses; though why they need be so large, to make the affair brilliant, since the guests were coming for charity, and not self-gratification, it might have been puzzling to tell.

But, as Cyril saw the preparations progress, he began to be troubled with one misgiving, — how was he to play his part in such an elegant affair, with any credit to himself or the occasion, in the plain and worn suit which was the best he possessed? He knew the glory of raiment in which most of his companions, who could afford to purchase the five-dollar tickets, would appear; and that many of them would have staid at home often, rather than be seen in such a suit as he had worn on occasions like this. And Cyril was growing exceedingly sensitive about his dress. He concluded, at last, that he had no right to be going where he could not furnish an attire suited to the grandeur of the occasion, and that he could not possibly act in the conspicuous position assigned him without a new evening suit. What then? Why, when Cyril had finished his decorating to his satisfaction, he could quietly withdraw from further labors, and delegate his duties for the evening to somebody else.

But Cyril could not resign himself to make the sacrifice. He argued that it would be impossible for him to do it; that his friends would leave him no peace, should he attempt to withdraw. Not another one of the managers had so extensive an acquaintance as he, or such a gift at creating, by his very presence, here and there, such a spirit of life and enjoyment throughout a room. His friends among his classmates counted it among their best chances for a pleasant evening, that he would be there. He already held quite a list of requests for introductions to this young lady or that, to whom no one could so favorably present his friends as he. Especially there was Tom. He shrank from ladies' society generally, but felt emboldened to present himself among them when the scene was only a public hall. The ceiling of a lady's drawing-room, though ever so lofty, was always oppressive to him, and the furniture was all stumbling-blocks; but he fancied he should move about the Music Hall more at his ease. And Tom, to the infinite amusement of his friends, had fixed an eye of admiration upon the daughter of one of the professors, a delicate and dainty maiden, upon whom the young man gazed in chapel, Sundays, to while away the tedious hours. A perfect pink she was for propriety, yet having, for all her demure elegance, some merry and mischievous spice in her disposition, that may have led her, when she perceived the steady stare of Tom's sober, scowling face in church, to cast at him just one or two bright glances that had bewitched him. At any rate, he stoutly averred that she had smiled at him, though all the fellows laughed incredulously at the story ; and so he had made Cyril promise him an introduction, and was getting himself up, " regardless," as his friends said, for the occasion. If he should learn that Cyril was going to fail him, what would be his wrath and disappointment! He would be content with nothing but the true reason ; and that Cyril did not want to give. If he did give it, Tom would offer to lend him money, and be angry if he did not take it. No, Cyril was sure he must go to the concert: he had proceeded too far to withdraw himself. But, the more he tried to be reconciled to the thought of going in his old clothes, the more impossible it seemed. So there he was, irresolute upon the three horns of his little dilemma: he could not have new clothes, he could not go in his old ones, and he could not stay away. Do not smile at his weakness in hesitating about so small a matter; for little temptations so often lead to great misfortunes and great sins. Recollect, it is not merely against flesh and blood that we fight, but against principalities and powers, against the rulers of the darkness of this world, against spiritual wickedness in high places; and do not fancy the armor of God — the breastplate of righteousness, the shield of faith, the sword of the Spirit — too cumbrous armor for such small occasions even as this : it was meant for just such, to be worn daily and hourly, and never put aside. Without it, Cyril was not safe.

When Cyril's mother had been looking over his wardrobe before he returned to college, she had said to him that she wished he might have a new suit : she knew well enough that he would often be tempted to wish for one himself. His father, who was sitting in the room apparently occupied with a book, heard the remark, though it had been made in a low tone not to reach his ear. " Well, mother," he said cheerfully, " we must certainly let Cyril have a new coat for the junior exhibition. I

CYRIL AT HOME.

recollect having my first broadcloth suit to wear on that day; and I kept it for state occasions for a long time afterward. We must contrive to get Cyril one then. It's becoming that a young man should be suitably dressed when he makes his first appearance in public."

These words now occurred to Cyril's mind, — " His first appearance in public ! " He could hardly help smiling at his father's innocence. His appearance upon the junior exhibition stage would be nothing for publicity compared with his appearance upon the floor of the Music Hall the night of the grand concert, or even compared with the part he had played in many a crowded drawing-room in the city before this. But, if he was to have a suit, why not have it now ? There would be no need of paying for it till spring, if that was more convenient for his father ; yet Cyril could still have it all winter, when he wanted it most. Should he write home, and tell his father of all these considerations ?

Ah ! Cyril could not do that : he dared not, when he thought of his father's pale face, and bent shoulders, and fast whitening hair. He knew the wrinkles of anxiety that would come upon the kind forehead, and the involuntary sigh the good man would send forth as he puzzled himself to excuse and gratify his son, turning over his resources in his mind, and, very likely, planning new work to supply the new wants; beginning his task of writing earlier in the morning, or continuing it later at night, to make time to produce something for publication; or a little lecture to deliver in some neighboring town to eke out his income, and make it cover this new expense. Cyril knew with what forebodings in her heart his mother would watch these doings, and remonstrate against them; and how his sisters would hold anxious consultations together again, looking around for the one forlorn resource for ministers' daughters, a school-teacher's place, in a country already overstocked with school-teachers. Ah, no! Cyril could not send home his wish: the wonder is, that, with such a remembrance, he could have cherished it at all. But all these thoughts were of interests absent, and distressed him only occasionally : they did not press upon him with the urgency of the ideas and examples that were at present surrounding him.

As the eventful evening drew near, he grew more and more excited about his part of the play. He became careless of restraints; it was as though he lived in a world where it was right for him to have what he pleased, to do as others did, without regard to the tyranny of circumstances. He said to himself, that he must have that suit at all events. It could be paid for in the spring: his father would most probably send the money then; and it was not worth while to trouble him about it at all at present. If Cyril should foresee any likelihood of his failing to send it, then, no doubt, he could contrive to pay it in some way himself. He might get classes to teach in some of the seminaries in town during his leisure hours. Once let this concert go by, so that he had again the use of his time and talents, and he could right his position quickly enough in some way. Surely, one with friends and ability like his need not be afraid to indulge in a little necessary expense like this. Whatever might happen, there was Tom Raddon, with his generous purse, that was sure to be at his friend's service, in case every thing else should fail.

It was Tom to whom Cyril said, one morning, as they sauntered to the post-office after recitation, —

"Raddon, I've got to get a new suit for that concert."

"You!" said Tom, apparently surprised. "Well, of course. I never thought of it though, because, somehow, you always look slick and bright enough at a party in your every-day clothes. Expect you're kind o' made for it; but we clumsy fellows have to be rigged up, like those stiff side-lights in the hall you had to tie up in evergreens to make 'em look festive."

"Well," said Cyril, "made for it or not, I can't be floor-manager in this old, rusty suit. So come in and introduce me to your tailor, to make him give me credit enough to trust me. I can't pay him right away."

" He'll be the better pleased, I reckon," growled Tom. " He'd never have the face to ask in cash for what he has the impudence to set down in the bill."

That was not encouraging to Cyril; but he said nothing. The two went into the tailoring establishment; and Cyril, having resolved to act without regard to right, was the more likely to be regardless of prudence, also. He turned over cloths, and inquired prices, as if he had been used to the frequent ordering of costly suits, and ended with choosing such material, and giving such directions, as would secure him such a suit as he fancied, without much consideration of the probable cost. The day of reckoning was some distance off: there would be plenty of time to think of it before it arrived.

Nevertheless, he did quake a little with dread when the elegant new suit came home; and he felt a sense of just shame, as though every one must know he had no right to wear it. The feeling was soon lost, however, in the excitement of the evening, and in gratified vanity, as he received the compliments and congratulations of his friends upon his improved appearance.

That night was, as had been promised, one long to be remembered in the annals of Eaton. The hall, when the finishing touches had been put to the decorations, and the gas was all lighted, exceeded in beautiful appearance all that Cyril had expected. Along the sides, flags and evergreens were wreathed above and below the finest paintings the private residences of the city could furnish for the occasion. Festoons were arched overhead; and from the center of the ceiling depended a magnificent basket of flowers, whose elegant pattern Cyril had himself designed.

The room began to be filled early; and the company was quite as large and brilliant as had been imagined. The ladies wore their gayest and most elegant dresses, and the gentlemen were not behind them in preparations for the festivity. The music had been brought from the neighboring metropolis, and was the best and most inspiriting. Its sweet strains, combined with the perfume of flowers, the bright light, and the animated throng of people, produced an effect that was upon many a young mind a sort of intoxication.

Cyril, whose name, connected with the admiration the decorations excited, was in every one's mouth, and whose appearance and manners entitled him to be called the most brilliant and noticeable young man in the room, heard snatches of complimentary talk about himself wherever he went. He did not show the elation he felt as he realized his position, except by the sparkle in his eye, and the brightness of his smile. He was busy enough in his share of the management, insuring the smooth and happy procedure of the programme. It was not his fault, that night, that any one to whom his graceful kindness could be made available did not enjoy the evening.

Nor did any thing occur to damp his own complacency till toward the close of the festivity. The crowd was fast thinning by the departure of the older and more sober portion of it, and Cyril had cast aside the cares of his office to join in the dancing. He was in the highest state of pleasurable excitement. He stood by his partner, waiting for the music of the quadrille to begin. Just then passed slowly by Tom Raddon, with the young lady upon his arm to whom Cyril had given the promised introduction, much fearing, nevertheless, that she would scorn the uncouth, over-dressed fellow. There was no doubt, however, that she had been kind and polite to him ; for Tom had followed her all the evening, claiming her every disengaged moment with a persistency in which a more accomplished gentleman would not have dared to indulge himself. And now, perhaps, as the easiest way of keeping up a conversation that would interest him, she had led Tom to talk about his everyday pursuits, his ways of managing life and study, his ordinary hopes and vexations. And in the progress of such stories he had informed her that to-morrow was the debating-day, and he was in no way prepared for it. And as they passed by Cyril she put this question, —

"What will you do, then, when you are called up ?"

"Oh! I shall be ready by that time," answered Tom rather boastfully. "You see, we fellows are so lucky as to have a good friend who knows about every thing, and was just born to string off words with a pen, so that they come to the right thing. He writes off something or other for each of us; and we study it at prayers, or on the way to breakfast: so, when the professor calls us up, we are pretty sure to have something to say."

Cyril's eyes turned in anxiety and wrath upon Tom, who did not perceive him. "The fool!" muttered Cyril to himself: "why couldn't he have better sense?"

The young lady was evidently interested, if not amused. Her lip had curled a little, contemptuously, and there was a sparkle either of fun or indignation in her eye, — Cyril could not have told which.

"Your friend is certainly very obliging," she said.

"Oh!" said honest Tom, "he don't do it for nothing. We wouldn't ask it of him: it's considerable work, you see. We pay him a dollar apiece for a composition."

"A dollar apiece!" said the young lady slowly; and Cyril could not mistake now the exceeding contempt in her voice and manner. "Is that the market-price for lies in Eaton University? Little enough, to be sure!"

Tom looked at her utterly confounded: the light had broken upon him too suddenly. She had spoken hastily upon an indignant impulse, as she often did upon a merry one, and, recovering herself, she said, half ashamed, "I beg your pardon!"

"What do you mean?" said Tom, dismayed at the consciousness of being under her rebuke.

She hesitated a minute between courtesy and the honest severity of her thought. "I mean," she said at last, her voice trembling with earnestness, "that I do not see how you can do such a thing as you have told me about. And I should think a man who could take pay for doing you such a service must be the meanest that ever lived. It is making and selling lies."

Tom turned scarlet with mortification at her rebuke, for Cyril's sake as well as his own.

Yet, in the midst of his confusion, Cyril heard him say with dogged faithfulness, "He is my friend," and for that forgave him the imprudence that had brought them the condemnation.

They passed by, and what they said more, or how they made peace with each other, Cyril could not tell. But for him the pleasure of the evening was gone. His head drooped, his figure lost its uprightness, under the burden of shame that seemed openly laid upon his shoulders. He hardly knew how he got through that dance, and answered his partner's chatting. He longed to be at liberty to hide himself in his room; but he was forced to keep his place till the most indefatigable of the dancers had tired themselves out, and the gray light of morning was at hand. People told him he looked tired; and tired and wretched enough he was. The staring reflection of himself that he met at every turn, from the many mirrors he had ordered placed around the room, was torturing to him in his consciousness of shame.

Returning at last to his room, he came upon Tom, pacing up and down the sidewalk before the door. Cyril opened it, and they went up together without a word. When he had lighted the lamp, he saw that Tom was very much excited; and Tom, perceiving, also, how tired and distressed Cyril looked, and having but one thought in his head at present, guessed the reason.

"Did you hear what she said?" he asked.

"Yes," answered Cyril.

"I say it was true, Rivers!" said Tom excitedly. "I'd like to kill myself to think how I showed myself without shame in telling that story!"

Cyril tried to bethink himself how he might quiet these self-reproaches, and send Tom away; for he wanted to be alone.

"Yes, what she said was true, Tom," he said; "and I am the one to be most ashamed. But it was not quite so bad as it looked to her. She did not know the circumstances, and she spoke too sharply, being hardly more than a stranger to you."

"I don't know," said Tom, "whether she spoke too sharply or not. I only know I took it kind of her. I wish you had spoken sharply: I shouldn't feel so mean, perhaps, as I do to-night."

Cyril was shaken by that blunt rebuke. He could make no answer.

"Why didn't you?" continued Tom, in his anger. "You pretend to know about these things; but I never was taught. I hardly know a lie is a lie when it concerns my getting what I want. But you might: why did you let anybody buy you into doing these things?"

Why, indeed? Cyril was utterly cowed by the question: he had not a word to say in self-defense. He sat looking into the fire with such a pale, harassed countenance, that Tom, in the midst of his wrath, noticed it, and was softened.

"Forgive me, old fellow!" he cried. "I had no business to blame you. You only meant to oblige us, and we all begged you to do it."

Cyril turned, and took some papers from the

table. Selecting one, he put it in Tom's hand. " It's the debate I wrote for you for to-morrow," he said.

With an angry jerk, Tom threw it into the fire; and that appeared to relieve him more than all his scolding.

" There ! " he said, the fierce scowl upon his face softening, as he watched the paper curl up in the blaze, " that does me good ! I shall be no liar to-morrow, if I do flunk. I believe I can go home and go to sleep upon that: it's time, I guess. Give me your hand, and say good-night, Rivers. If I said any thing unkind, forgive me before I go."

He went away, and left Cyril still sitting by the fire. He was utterly exhausted; but he would not try to rest. His mind was dazed by all the events of the evening, — the exciting scenes with which it had begun; the sharp, true words that had cut short its pleasure; Tom's reproaches; and the jealous surprise with which he discovered that one whom he had judged it impossible to lead from selfish wrong-doing had awakened, at a few words from a stranger, to a deeper sense of shame and repentance than Cyril himself could feel. His mind ran back and forth over these things, and then to his new clothes, unpaid for, and then to his home, and sick father. He was too much exhausted to view any of the circumstances of his situation clearly; but they appeared to him such, that he was filled with unutterable depression, shame, and grief.

He sat in his chair, absorbed in anxious and uneasy thoughts, till the morning twilight brightened, and the college rising-bell roused him to the fact that another day had begun. He rose and changed his dress, and bathed his face and hands. The half-dozen debates he had finished, with Tom's, for some of his classmates, were lying upon the table. What should he do with them? Follow Tom's example, and throw them into the fire? He took them up and hesitated. They had been promised, and their loss would cause disappointment. The fellows depended upon them: it would not be fair to break his promise about them. But he would never do a thing of the kind again : he had received sufficient warning, surely, of the insecurity of such conduct. That story might easily now come to the professors' ears, and Cyril could see how it would appear to any one whose moral sense was not blunted by the constant contact with such dishonest dealings. Oh, no! he could not do the thing again.

He sat down to look over some lesson, trying to restore himself to his usual frame of mind. The beginning of the day's routine, and soon the society of those over whose thoughts and feelings had come no change since yesterday, helped him. By ten o'clock, when he went into the debating-class, all the experiences of the past night seemed hardly more than a dream, the shadow of a cloud that had come and gone in an hour. He could hear Benson speaking his false essay, with only a momentary twinge of fear and shame. And the morning sunshine had almost the same effect upon Tom. He half repented burning the essay Cyril had prepared for him, and amused the fellows about him by telling the story, and pretending to growl over his folly. Yet, after all, he was more glad than sorry. There remained enough of bitterness about the thought of this deception to keep both himself and Cyril from practicing it again.

CHAPTER XI.

THE UNFAITHFUL STEWARD.

"Thorns and snares are in the way of the froward."

FEW days of quiet, that followed the promenade concert, restored Cyril to some measure of wisdom. He saw that it behooved him to be in earnest in finding means to pay the debt he had incurred; and he actually set on foot inquiries, through his tutors and other friends, for a place where his services as teacher during some hours of the day might earn him some income. But he met with no immediate success in his efforts; and as they had been made reluctantly, through necessity, he did not follow them up very persistently. His attention was soon distracted by some new gayety like that through which he had just passed.

Elated again by pleasure and vanity, again he lost sight of his responsibilities; and so up and down, from the top of one wave of excitement, through intervals of uncomfortable anxiety, to another, he drifted through the winter, till, with a heart that had no welcome for the approaching season, he discovered that March had brought in the spring.

As I approach the *dénouement* of my story, I am troubled with wondering whether I have prepared the way for it, so that it will not seem unnatural and startling. But perhaps I can not expect to do that, since I can only tell it as it occurred; and it was startling to those who knew Cyril best. We may see the tall tree sway in the wind, down to its very roots, and be sure that some day the blast will overthrow it; but when the crash comes, though long awaited, it nevertheless fills the beholder with amazement and regret.

There was a new melodeon wanted at the Bethel Mission; and it had been voted that funds for its purchase should be collected as speedily as possible, and placed in the hands of the treasurer, who was instructed, as soon as he had a sufficient amount, to select and pay for the instrument. Cyril accepted the charge as lightly as he had done many another of the same kind that had fallen among the duties of his office. With that sort of enthusiasm and ambition which he had often shown before in gaining something for the school, — but perhaps more from the desire to please the little band of teachers with whom he was already so popular, than from any principle in forwarding a good cause, — he set about doing his share to collect the sum necessary. He had brought a good deal of money into the school since his connection with it, although he had so little to contribute himself. There were enough among his classmates carelessly throwing money about, whose benevolent impulses he could reach by his persuasive statement of the claims of this charity He was as successful this time as always. He had laid Tom under contribution, — who, in these days, was growing wonderfully tractable to good influences, — and others beside: and the exertions of the rest of the teachers, added to Cyril's, had almost gained the sum needed.

But, beside this little interest with which he was momentarily occupying his thoughts in the pause of sports at the breaking-up of the winter, there were other matters, far more closely concerning Cyril, that were all the time weighing upon his mind, and very nearly distracting him with their entanglements.

First of all, there was news from home that his father's infirm state of health had ended in an alarming illness. Next, there was Cyril's debt. The bill for his suit had been sent in: and the merchant, who had had some unfortunate experience in dealing with students, would be likely to press his claim with unpleasant urgency before he allowed Cyril to go home for vacation without making payment. Whether he did or not, however, Cyril's knowledge of his inability to pay was becoming a constant torture to him. He felt the utmost reluctance to write to his mother, reminding her of his father's promise of a new suit for the approaching exhibition; but no other resource seemed left him.   Lastly, there was the dissertation, which he must prepare for that occasion, and which must make up in brilliancy for what his appointment lacked in rank; and, distracted by other cares, it seemed to him, in his first attempts to begin writing, that his own particular genius and facility had forsaken him. He could not even think of any subject for his essay that seemed in the least attractive. He had already put off attending to it till but little time was left; and now, irresolute, and wandering in thought from one topic to another, finding nothing pleasing in any, he had never felt in such despair over any task before.

Driven by necessity, however, he at last fixed upon a subject; and, with a pile of books to be examined for information, he shut himself into his room one Saturday afternoon, determined to finish some plan of his undertaking before nightfall. He entered upon his work in good earnest; and was at last beginning to concentrate his straying thoughts, and even to become interested, when he was interrupted by a gentle rap upon his door. He paid no heed at first, supposing that some student neighbor was there, who, not being answered, would take it for granted that his classmate was not at home, and so pass on. But, the knock being repeated, Cyril raised his head, and said, " Go on, if you please, fellows. I'm busy, you see. I can't let you in just now."

But instead of some hearty voice calling " All right !" in answer, and the sound of noisy feet clattering down stairs, some one, not young certainly, gave a dry, quiet cough, and an " Ahem !" and a voice that Cyril did not recognize said respectfully, —

" I'm sorry to disturb you, Mr. Rivers ; but I should like to speak with you a minute."

Of course, Cyril, though very reluctant, rose, and opened the door. There stood a little man with very black eyes and hair, and fashionably-cut whiskers, with a somewhat Jewish cast of countenance, and arrayed, from the top of his shining beaver to the pointed tips of his shining boots, in the very latest and neatest style of dress. Why did Cyril start,

and look so exceedingly dismayed, at the sight
of this little man, who was not a gentleman,
certainly, for all his fine dress, and who was
bowing to him so politely? Alas! he owed
him money. He had taken his goods, and
worn them, without making payment. It was
as though Cyril Rivers, so proud and sensitive,
the pet of refined society, the very gentleman
of his class, was now dependent upon the
charity of this little Jewish-looking merchant-
tailor, who had come to remind him of his
degradation, perhaps cunning enough to know
that this was the surest way of obtaining the
payment of his claim. As he began with
bland civility to explain why he had been
forced to intrude upon Mr. Rivers again with
his little bill, Cyril felt his position to be too
intolerable to be borne. To deny the man,
to be obliged to ask his patience and forbear-
ance a little longer, to be forced to be explicit
in telling the circumstances that had disappointed him in his hope of making payment,
falsifying statements to make his case fairer,
and all for a man he despised, and now even

hated, because he had the advantage, was what Cyril could not do. He felt his cheeks burning, and his tongue palsied in his mouth, with the angry obstinacy with which his pride rose up against his necessity. He was not used to being dunned, you see. He was not hardened to such situations. Try to put yourself in his place, young people who read this, and who never yet have known the irksomeness of debt, and you will not so much wonder at what he did.

There was money enough in his pockets; not his own, but in his trust. The temptation was too strong; the impulse that drove him to yield to it, too blind and headstrong. Let come what would, he would be free from such a miserable care as this. The money for the melodeon would not be wanted immediately: there would be time to make it good. There was his father's promise of new clothes, that might yet be fulfilled; there was, at any rate, Tom's friendship and wealth to fall back upon. Only let him get rid of this man's claim: no other could possibly be so galling. Quick as a flash, these thoughts passed through Cyril's mind. He pulled forth his treasurer's purse, and, counting out sixty dollars as proudly and indifferently as if they had been all his own, put them into the tailor's hand. The little man, somewhat surprised, but very well pleased to get his money, smiled and bowed, and thanked Mr. Rivers for his patronage, and detailed a long list of elegant new spring goods, which he wished the young gentlemen would only come in and examine.

But, when he had gone, do you think Cyril returned to his writing with quiet mind? Ah, no! Mechanically he seated himself at the table, and opened his book, to find himself, in a few moments, trembling from head to foot, his hands refusing to obey him, his eyes unable to make out the letters upon the page, his mind in a maze of fears. He rose, and walked up and down the room, trying to steady his thoughts, to look at his case fairly, to count up the chances for and against him, to form some plan of action. What was this he had done? how came he to do it? and how was he to manage the consequences? He tried to think and plan, and could not. He tried to comfort himself, and grew the more terrified.

There was no more writing for him 'that afternoon. In a sort of desperation, he took his hat, and went down to the post-office. He would surely have a letter from his mother to-night, and that might relieve him. He knew the evening mail was not in yet; but he was driven by consuming anxiety to go and linger about the doors of the post-office, that his turn might come first in the distribution. There were several of his classmates loitering about there, up and down the busy street, to kill time, not knowing what else to do with the Saturday afternoon. They hailed him with wonder. "What! you down here, Rivers?" they cried. "You shut yourself up to write your essay!"

Cyril joined them. He seemed in his gayest mood, though he was pale, and had a worn, tired look. He would not for the world have had any one know how fear preyed upon his heart. Some one proposed going to a neighboring billiard-saloon to while away the time till the mail came in. Cyril, from motives of prudence, and for want of taste for the game, had heretofore kept away from such places; but he yielded readily enough now to the request. He tried joining in the game; but he could pay no more attention to it than he had been able to give to his writing. His misplay utterly astonished his companions, even in a beginner. "I should think you were drunk, Rivers," said one. But it was not wine, but intolerable suspense, that had taken away Cyril's control over his thoughts and actions. He soon gave up trying to play, and spent the time in walking up and down the room, till, from the window, he saw the mail-wagon drive up opposite. Quick as a flash, he was out of the room, down stairs, and across the street.

With what trembling he asked for his letter! It was there, sure enough, with the home postmark, and in his mother's writing. He stepped aside to the window to tear open the envelope and discover the contents. First of all, he saw there was no check within; and then with a sinking heart, in the selfishness of fear, he ran his eye over the loving lines, heedless of all they would impart, till he came to the one piece of information that seemed most to concern him now. The tenderness with which it was conveyed, the disappointment and anxiety of the writer, touched him not at all at this moment. He only gathered that neither father nor mother could help him. His father's sickness did not seem to alarm him, nor his mother's grief and foreboding to distress him. There was but one thought in his mind at this crisis: How was he to save himself from public disgrace?

He could think of but one resource, and that was in Tom's friendship. There had been a sort of separation between Tom and Cyril since the night of the promenade concert. It was not an estrangement of the heart; for, when they met, their intercourse was still very kindly. But there was a certain embarrassment in it not like the old freedom. Cyril, with the proud shyness of one who felt that the friend who once trusted him had at last discovered his weakness, could not advise or good-naturedly take the command of Tom as he used to do; and Tom, still loving Cyril, but not confident in him as heretofore, could not hide the change in his feelings. Moreover, Tom was changed to all. Some new influence had come over him this winter. He had been trying hard to be more studious; but his demeanor was variable. Sometimes he would seem exceedingly quiet and earnest, full of moral and reflective remarks that astonished and amused his friends, but sometimes restless and discontented, savagely quarreling with himself and every thing about him.

But Cyril was still sure that he might trust Tom's loving generosity toward himself, and tried to fortify himself with that assurance in his present distress of mind.

He had one more ordeal to go through before he could see Tom and set his mind at rest on this point. To-night there was to be another teachers' meeting. It would be torture to Cyril to meet those whose trust he had betrayed; but his anxiety would not let him stay away. He would be expected to-night to report about the funds for the melodeon, and to receive additions to them; no doubt, to have the means placed at his disposal to procure the instrument during the coming week.

He appeared at the meeting as animated and as self-confident as if no feeling of uneasiness and guilt and shame had ever visited his heart. He gave in his report of funds raised for the melodeon, with a great show of pleasure at the speed with which they had been collected. He said, boldly, that only fifteen dollars remained to be gathered before the school would be enabled to make such a purchase as was desired. As he had partly anticipated, the sum was at once contributed among those present; and there was apparently nothing now to prevent the unfortunate Cyril from buying the instrument during the coming week.

He had, some time previously, asked Miss Kerlie to give him the benefit of her judgment in the choice of the melodeon: so now, with untroubled face, he went and asked her to fix a day when she could go with him to make the purchase ; glad enough, however, that she placed it as far on in the week as the following Thursday. With four days' respite, and with a little comfort in realizing how utterly unimagined yet was his deed of this afternoon, he went home, already grown somewhat harder and bolder in bearing his hidden guilt.

But he could not sleep until he had seen Tom. He went from the teachers' meeting to Tom's room ; but, discovering from the sounds of voices that his friend was not alone, he walked restlessly up and down the street till he saw Tom's guests come out together. Then Cyril went and rapped upon the door, saying, " Can I come in, Tom ?   It is Rivers."

" Come in," answered Tom.

Cyril entered, to find the room full of smoke, through which he dimly discerned Tom sitting by the table, bending his head over his books. There was a vexed scowl upon his face. His Plato, and his grammars and lexicons and " ponies," were all strewed about him. Cyril was too much surprised at the sight to restrain his comment.

" What! studying on Saturday night ? "

He had not known Tom to do such a thing since he had been in college. That Sunday was the only day in the week proper to get lessons in, had been, apparently, a main point in Tom's creed; but Cyril saw at once that he had made a mistake in noticing this change of habits.

" Why not ? " said Tom defiantly. And then, too proud to yield to a little false shame about his motives, he added, " Because I've been a heathen all my life, is that a reason why I shouldn't try to be better ? I tell you, I haven't forgot what Stavens said once about one law for us all, saints and heathens together."

Cyril, yet more surprised, hastened to soothe him. The slight sarcasm vanished from his face; and some of the sorrow that was in his heart appeared instead, as he sat down beside Tom, and answered him gently, —

" You know I'm glad, Tom. It's a hundred times better to keep it. And don't suppose I thought it strange you should try to do it. You call yourself a heathen, and think I must be better, because I have been trained up in religious ways. I tell you, I never felt any right to ask you to join me in them, I was so much worse in them than you in your kind of life. You know some of the miserable things I've done: but if you knew all, you would despise me; you would see as I do, plainly enough, which of us is the most likely to do right."

It eased Cyril's mind to make this confession; but its truth was concealed by the disguise of humility and over-scrupulousness to a partial eye. Tom's friendship warmed as he perceived Cyril's sadness, and heard this self-depreciation. He refused to believe words like those.

"Don't talk so, Rivers!" he said. "We all get wrong living here together. We don't think; and we do what is bad without knowing or caring, because nobody else seems to know or care. Talk of yourself! Why, just think of me in comparison: think what an idle, wasteful, vicious, fool's life I've lived here! It makes me curse myself now. I can't tell you how I've come to see it; but I do see it: and the worst is, I can't get out of it. I try and try, and am back in it before I know it. I thought I would try and get some good out of to-morrow, as some other folks seem to ; but I sha'n't make it out. It'll be the old story. If I try to listen in chapel, it'll all seem a dreary jargon, that I don't understand; and very likely I shall go to sleep. And then, out of chapel, you know how time goes when the fellows get together. By night, I shall be enough disgusted with my trying, to give it up, and do any thing they tease me to do. What can I do? Sometimes I wish I never had been born."

Alas that Cyril had never fought the good fight himself! — had never himself kept the faith! Here was offered him the opportunity of doing a work, which having done, a man might die contented, — a work which would have made his soul shine as the stars, for ever and ever. Tom's was the old cry, " What shall I do to be saved ? " raised in confidence to one whom he loved. If Cyril could have answered it out of the fervor of faith in his own heart, if he could have directed this seeking, struggling spirit toward the Light upon which his own eyes had been fixed, he might now have saved a soul from death.

But, alas! his own hands had put such blessedness out of his reach. He had never truly loved God's service; and he was not thinking now of that or of poor Tom's welfare, but of himself, — of his own difficulties and trials. He was to help himself, not Tom; and again he failed his friend, crying " Peace, peace!" when there was no peace. He told Tom to keep on trying, and that, as he grew older, he would become more settled, and correct in his desires; that the strife within him between good and evil inclinations would gradually cease as his character matured : as if in all a man's life such a thing could be, unless either God forsook him, or grace reigned triumphant within him. Surely Cyril must have known better than this; but the truth he once thought he believed he felt no more.

Such comfort might have been true, for all Tom could tell; but it left him unsatisfied.

He knew not what he had longed for; but surely this was not it. He ceased to talk about himself, and there was a short silence between them.

At last, Cyril offered to help him with his lesson; but he declined the offer in a manner almost surly.

"No," said he. "It's time I stood alone, or else fell out of my class. Sometimes I think I wouldn't care if I was dropped, and my father got tired of spending for me, and left me to take care of myself, if I only could keep out of this cursed cheating."

Then there was another silence, till Cyril in his sin, seeming to see this last friend separating from him in his newly-awakened conscientiousness, showed such sadness in his face as he sat looking into the fire, that Tom, noticing at last, was startled.

"What ails you, old fellow?" he asked fondly.

"I'm in trouble, Tom. I came over here to ask you to help me out."

"What is it, then? You know I'll do it if I can."

Cyril hesitated a moment; and, when he answered, he could not help giving a false coloring to his necessity.

"Tom," he said at last, "I have been disappointed. That suit I got last winter, I got without my father's knowledge, because he had promised me one this spring; and I thought I could pay as well now as then. But father is sick, and they can not let me have the money; and Ragye is dunning for what I owe him. I can't endure it any longer. I want you to lend me sixty dollars, and trust me — I don't know how long, perhaps two or three years — to pay it. You see, I can't trouble my father now: he is sick, — pretty nearly worked and worried to death."

"Ragye!" said Tom in great wrath. "Dunning, is he? The impudent scoundrel! Why didn't you kick him down stairs? The little low-lived tailor! I'd like to see him dun me! Why, he's only waited four months! I'll go down and blow him up for his impudence myself!"

"Don't you do it, Tom!" Cyril cried in

terror. "Blow him up on your own account if you like; but this is my business. I can't wrangle with tradesmen; but I'm wretched when I'm in their debt. Lend me the money if you can, dear fellow; but don't go talking to Ragye about my affairs."

"But," said Tom, looking very sorry, "I haven't got the money, Rivers. I've spent almost to my last dollar; and father will not send me more than enough at the end of the term to pay up and get home with. Only if you wait till then, I guess I can persuade him to send me sixty more. I'll write, and try."

Cyril groaned: he felt faint with the oppression of dismay. "It won't do, Tom," said he: "I want it now. I'm worn out with thinking of this thing."

"But you needn't be," said Tom, puzzled. "I'll go down and tell Ragye, if he so much as hints about your bill again, he'll forfeit my custom. Between us, we can get the money in plenty of time to pay him."

But, seeing that Cyril still remained uncomforted, he asked, after a minute, earnestly, "What else *can* I do for you, Rivers?".

"Nothing," said Cyril, rising; "but please don't do that, Tom. Thank you all the same, though. Never mind about it: don't trouble yourself about it any more. I'll settle it myself. I'll go back to my room, and give you a chance to get your lesson. Good-night!"

Tom looked wonderingly after him as he departed. "It is strange," Tom said to himself. "He is quiet, and never brags; but he's as proud as a prince. How nervous and angry he was when I offered to speak to Ragye! One would think I meant to beg the tailor for him. Poor Rivers! I wish he had the money my father gives me: he'd spend it like a prince, not like a loafer as I do, never having any thing to lend a friend in trouble. And, as for me, I wish I had been poor, and had to work hard all my life. I believe it would have been better for such a great stupid as I. What business have I to be in purple and fine linen? It's like dressing an ox up in 'em: the yoke and the harness would be better for him."

Ah, foolish Tom! like many another discon-

tented youth, finding fault with the allotments
of Providence; unwilling to see the yoke and
the harness laid ready for you; not knowing
that whether it be rough, or whether it be
padded, it must be best for you because it is
yours, or that it must grow light and easy for
you if accepted because it is His.

Poor Cyril has, with his eyes open as it
were, cast away his yoke for a garland of
flowers, that now, strange to say, begins to
weigh upon him like a chain, pressing poison-
ous, torturing thorns into his very heart.

Alone in his room again, Cyril walked up and
down, unable to decide what measure to take
next. There was one thing he could do: if
he should write and tell his mother all, in her
terror at the thought of his disgrace, he knew
she would contrive in some way to raise the
sixty dollars of which he stood in need; and
then, he said to himself, he would leave
college at the end of the term, and work night
and day to repay her doubly. To let her help
him, would, no doubt, be the easiest way out
of his difficulty; but I am thankful Cyril had

manliness enough not to avail himself of it. Why should he cast the penalty of his folly and sins upon his feeble mother, already struggling with so many anxieties? — make her suffer the unspeakable bitterness of discovering how weak and worthless was the son of whom she had been so proud? Cyril was not quite selfish enough for that. He felt, that, since he had incurred the trouble, he must make his way out of it alone.

There was another and a better course suggested to his mind. It was, since he had done wrong which he could in no way repair, to go and confess it. Would he not do wisely to go to-night to John Seelye, that good and true man, whose trust in bringing him into the school he had so violated, and tell him all, and ask and follow his advice? However humiliating such a course, it would at least be the speediest way for Cyril to get back to honorable conduct. However low he might be brought in the sight of others, he need not scorn himself so bitterly any more; and to bring upon himself all the reprobation he

JOHN SEELYE'S QUESTION.

dreaded seemed better than to suffer longer the haunting fear of it. The momentary impulse was so strong, that Cyril even laid his hand upon the door to go in search of John; and then his pride arrested him. It was late, he said to himself. He need not go to-night: he could wait till Monday. And then he grew suddenly bold with a new thought. Why need he go at all? There was no such desperation in his case as he had been persuading himself. If the melodeon must be bought next week, it need not be paid for then. The school and its conductors were well known, and could easily obtain credit. He would make a first visit to the shop before he took Miss Kerlie there; and no doubt he could make some arrangement with the proprietor to let the payment rest till some future time. This thought freed him from immediate anxiety, so that at last he could lie down to rest. But his sleep was disturbed; his unforgiven sins, and the troubles in which they had involved him, haunted him in his dreams.

CHAPTER XII.

ALONE IN THE LIBRARY.

" As a bird hasteth to the snare, and knoweth not that it is for his
life."

CYRIL awoke the next morning confirmed in his foolish resolves; greater confidence in himself, and greater fear of confession, coming with the daylight. He said to himself that he had been foolish to be so much disturbed; that he had done nothing so very terrible, — nothing that he could not repair without its being known to any one.

But, in spite of his confident reasoning, he was not himself when the week began. He brought a pre-occupied mind to all his duties; a mind that was turning over and over its hidden thought of trouble and shame, and planning, again and again, every step of its scheme of escape. Weary as he might be of the remembrance of his deed, he could not turn away his eyes from viewing and reviewing its every detail; however, he tried to forget himself in pleasure and in application.

At the first possible moment he went down to the melodeon factory, feeling that, if the necessary falsehood were once told, he should be more at rest.

With a quiet manner, and an observant eye, he went through the warerooms, trying this instrument and that, as though intent upon nothing but making the best choice, yet all the while revolving in his mind how to propose the terms of purchase he was obliged to offer. At last, after having pretty thoroughly examined the stock, he pointed out two or three of the instruments as those among which his choice would probably be; explaining that he wished to bring a lady to examine them, and help him make the final decision. "But first," he said, "I must explain to you the circumstances under which I am making this purchase. I am acting for the Bethel-mission Sunday

School, the name of which must be familiar to
you. We have the funds for the purpose
pledged; but the money is not yet in hand,
and may not be for some weeks. Meanwhile,
our old instrument being badly broken, we are
much inconvenienced for want of one. Are
you willing to let us have this, and trust us a
while for its payment? I am the treasurer,
and will give my name in pledge for the in-
debtedness."

"With perfect willingness," answered the
merchant. "It is all the same to us, sir. You
can pay at your own convenience."

"Very well, then," said Cyril. "Expect
me here again in a few days."

And, upon Thursday, Miss Kerlie and he
went together, and after much discussion, found
the *chef d'œuvre* of all the instruments in the
shop for the price agreed upon; and it was
readily sent to the chapel, and set up in its
place, without another word to Cyril about its
cost.

And now he hoped the matter was fairly off
his mind for a while, and that he might enjoy a

brief respite from thinking over it. But, instead of that, he seemed to grow the more uneasy and wretched. He set himself desperately at work upon his dissertation, the time for the delivery of which was drawing fatally near. But if he had never taken pen in hand before, or put word after word upon paper, he thought he could not have found himself more unable to write. Thought was paralyzed ; reflection had fled beyond the reach of any summons ; memory was empty of the ghost of an idea. He had never had such an experience before. Let the subject be what it might, when he had set himself to consider it, he could usually find enough of interest in it to set his thoughts flowing, and to put him into a fervent energy to express them. But now the powers of his mind seemed to have rebelled against him. Disheartened and disgusted, he pushed on, by force of will and necessity, a feeble and unworthy work, that, a month ago, he would not have been willing to call his own. The knowledge of his ill success, instead of spurring him to greater effort, seemed to distract and paralyze him the more. He longed, with all that was left of his ambition as a student, to do himself credit on this occasion. He foresaw, that, unless his father's health improved, this might be his last year at college; and he wanted to leave some honorable reputation behind for all the promise with which he had entered. He was dismayed and wretched to discover his powerlessness.

Ah! a clear conscience is the best security for a clear head. Perfect control over the faculties of the mind, and the highest vigor of those faculties, can not be expected by one who is indulging or hiding sin. A man's powers must be all disordered and crippled when Satan is leading him captive at his will. Let such a man expect dimness of vision, and trembling hands, and a failing heart.

The news from home distracted poor Cyril with another cause for fear. They wrote that his father's state forbade any of the family from coming to hear their dear Cyril speak at the exhibition; and his mother bade him hurry home as soon as it was over. He wrote, and begged her leave to go now; telling her some of his trouble in writing his essay, and giving as a reason his extreme anxiety about his father. But she answered, that his father would be more disturbed by his return home before the term closed than benefited by his presence; that he must stay and do his work with as much credit to himself as possible; and that the thought of his sick father, instead of being a hinderance to him, must give him double earnestness in his effort. From such letters, Cyril would return again to his task, shortly to find himself wondering whether Tom would succeed in obtaining that sixty dollars from his father, and how soon it would come; or whether the melodeon merchant might, by any chance, let out the secret of the charge to any one connected with the Sunday school; or what he could do to earn the money during the coming vacation. For such thoughts he called himself a fool and a coward; but that did not help him to banish his folly and cowardice.

The days passed by all too quickly, though they were so miserable. In them Cyril was

very much changed. He shrank from companionship, pleading the necessity of industry
upon his essay. He was as silent and spiritless as
he had been used to be vivacious and enthusiastic. He grew pale and sad-looking; but,
when he was questioned, he found sufficient
excuse for that in mentioning his father's illness.

It wanted but a week of the day when the
essays were to be handed in for revision. It
was late on Saturday afternoon. Cyril had
been drudging over his forced and unsatisfactory labor until he was nearly worn out. In
despair at the confusion in his mind, and the
failure of his memory when he tried to recollect some line of argument he was citing from
a work he had read, he laid down his pen,
feeling that he must go again to the college
library to find the volume and give the passage
a fresh perusal. It was past the hour for the
closing of the library; but the state of his
work seemed to admit of no delay. He hoped,
too, the short walk in the open air, and the
few moments' change of employment, might re-
fresh and clear his mind.

He went, therefore, to the librarian's room, and, stating the urgency of the case, begged the use of the keys. His request seemed reasonable; and his statement of being hard at work was proved by his anxious, tired face. He assured the librarian that he could lay his hand upon the book in a minute; and the keys were intrusted to him without any hesitation.

Cyril opened the doors of the great hall of books, and turned the key in the lock behind him. He was all alone in the lofty, silent room. Spring sunlight streamed in through the western windows high above the tiers of books, and filled the arched vaults of the ceiling full of yellow light. Below, in silent whiteness, the busts of great and good men who had helped rear this treasure-house of thought stood for ever on guard to protect its sanctity. Behind them, in ranks of thousands, shelf above shelf, along the walls, were ranged the volumes of the wisdom of all ages. Their lettered backs gleamed down upon Cyril with lines of light from far above reach, — lines like the glitter of lightning along dark clouds that were full of promises of blessing to the thirsty soul.

Cyril stood and looked about him, awe and quietness stealing over his vexed spirit. He always liked to be here. The common world, with all that was mean and violent and sorrowful in it, seemed shut out. The windows were so far up, they showed only the clouds and blue sky. Whatever of men's lives had been brought into this chamber was the best part, — the choice fruit of knowledge won by labor; wisdom distilled from the experience of sorrow; the clear cry of warning wrung out by the bitter knowledge of sin, but not the labor and sorrow and foul sin themselves. So, moreover, it seemed as if whoever visited this place left behind him his weaker self, and appeared at his best and noblest, to be like the company in which he found himself. If he were young, he forgot the vanity which occupied his thoughts outside, and grew grave in countenance, looking about him with momentary earnestness for help toward some higher and more rarely-heeded aim; if he were old, he forgot anxiety, and grew peaceful at heart in this quiet company. Shall I speak too highly of this library-hall, filled by wise and careful judgment, when I see in it some dim likeness of that holy house to which we all are called? For here are gathered the spirits of just men, if not yet made perfect, yet in their most perfect earthly attainment; here are an innumerable company, if not of angels, yet of thoughts whispered by angels to souls that always waited listening; here is not, indeed, the glorious presence of the Mediator of the new covenant, yet there are to be found here the results of the light and love and knowledge that have been growing and increasing in all parts of the world from the establishment of that covenant with men. Walk softly here, then, and subdue your souls to purity and reverence, as in a sacred spot.

In this place, so silent, so pleasant, so almost solemn, Cyril was alone; not with exactly such thoughts as I have written above, but first with a sense of peace at just being alone. He almost wished he need never go forth again into the world he had sinned against, and whose condemnation he dreaded. His own room swarmed with harassing regrets and dreads: there was no solitude there ; but here they did not follow him. He believed, if he might come here to write, he could soon finish the essay over which he had spent so much labor in vain. He was at ease here ; he was himself again. And with this feeling of solitude came a sense of power. The great doors were locked, and he held the keys. The windows were high up : no eye could behold him. All things within the room were at his undisturbed command.

He felt in no haste now to attend to his errand. He walked slowly along the room, stopping to look musingly upon the strong or noble features of the marble likenesses, or to ponder, with childish, curious wondering, the tablets of stone, covered with hieroglyphics, that had been brought from ruined cities thousands of years old. He was so glad to forget himself for a little while, to hide himself within these stone walls, ivy-covered and book-lined, from the pursuit of fear and the urging of necessity ! He knew just where to find the volume in search of which he had come ; but, instead of hastening toward that corner, he seemed to keep away from it. He sauntered into alcoves where he had never been before ; taking down and examining ancient volumes pierced through by the progress of the little book-worm as by a shot, or meddling with parchment manuscripts removed from the hand of the transcriber by centuries of time.

At last, a little gallery overhead in a recess attracted his attention. Heaps of pamphlets covered with dust appeared to be stowed away there. There was no ascent from the library-hall to that gallery ; but Cyril was seized with a strange desire to explore it. He did not stop to consider, that, by all this loitering and meddling, he was betraying the trust reposed in him ; to say nothing of the fact, that, by all this idle delay, he risked destroying the labor of the afternoon in the concentration of his thought upon the work he had left to come here. He took the steps used for reaching the high shelves, and placed them against the side of the recess across which the gallery bridged. Standing upon them, he could reach the banister above with his hand. He was active enough with the help of that, and the edge of a shelf that offered another step for his foot, to make the ascent; and, yielding to an idle impulse, he swung himself up, climbed over the railing, and stood among the dusty heaps of papers. What thing of interest he expected to find there, he could not have told: he hardly cared to examine what was in the place now he had reached it. There were collections of pamphlets filed in orderly manner, each file labeled so as to show the nature of its contents; there were the annual catalogues of the college for many years; there were memorial sermons about great men connected with the institution, and the preachers' memorial sermons above those. Last of all, Cyril came upon a great heap of such orations of students as had been thought worthy of being kept in published form, — pamphlets that had been accumulating during many years.

These, the efforts of young men like himself, — like himself too, no doubt, once accounted brilliant, possessed of more than ordinary talent, and likely to win more than ordinary reputation, yet most of whom had somehow missed fame and a great career, as something in his heart seemed to assure him that he should do, — interested Cyril. He took up one and another of the little books, read its title and its date, the name of the author, and a paragraph or two ; saying sadly to himself as he laid each one aside, " I could do as well as that, or better, if I could only do my best. If I were only myself again ! I have not found one here whose work shows powers superior to mine."

Such comparisons seemed to soothe the mortification he suffered in his present disability.

At last, he drew forth a pamphlet which attracted him by bearing a name familiar to his ears, — a name beginning to be celebrated ; that of a writer whose works had always given Cyril special delight. His interest was greatly increased, as he read the subject of the oration (now twenty years old), to find it very similar to the one he had chosen for his own. With eagerness he opened the pamphlet, and began to read.

He drew a long sigh of pleasure and sympathy as he read the first paragraph. He was struck with the similarity of the style and mode of thought here shown to his own in his happiest moments. The surprise this feeling gave him was increased as he read. It was as if here was what he had been vainly striving to reach in thought, written out nobly and fully, just as he had longed to write it. Here were signs of a mind exceedingly like his own, possessed of the same age, the same knowledge almost, the same tastes, and ways of thought and feeling, but opening under better influences, — the influences to which Cyril had once hoped to give himself up, but from which he had suffered little sins to separate him, — the influences of God's enlightening Spirit ever sought and obeyed. As he read on, and recognized this, Cyril's pleasure turned to regret and envy that were bitter in his heart.

But, before he could finish the piece, it grew too dark in that dark recess for him to read longer. But he could not leave that pamphlet. He replaced all the rest as he had found them ; but this he put in his breast-pocket, bent upon examining it more at his leisure. He was not afraid to abstract it from its place, from which, in all probability, it would never be missed. He confessed to himself no mean intent in taking it ; but as he descended, and put the ladder back in its place, he seemed as eager to hasten away from the spot as he had been pleased to linger there a few moments before. The great room had grown dreary in the gathering dusk ; the dark walls frowned upon him, and the ghostly busts stared at him with their blank eyes with severe and stony gaze. He would have gone away without the book for which he had come, but that he remembered, as he closed the door, that he might be questioned about it when he returned the keys. He hastened back, but could not find it as easily as he had supposed, it was growing so dark. He grew nervous in the search, and his hands trembled, as at last he pulled the volume down from its shelf. He hurried away, glad to be out of the room, which seemed not lonely now, but full of spirits that whispered together, prophesying harm, and saying of him bitter and reproachful things.

He carried back the keys, making some plausible excuse for his stay in the library. By this time, the supper-bell was ringing; and after that came the teachers' meeting, from which he seemed nervously afraid to stay away. It was half-past nine before he was again alone in his room, ready to take up his writing. He read over what he had accomplished, more than ever dissatisfied with it, angry with himself for his failure, and desperate at thinking that the end of the task seemed farther off than when he began. He sat a while in moody thought, and then, taking from his pocket the oration he had brought from the library, slowly perused it again, drawing comparisons between it and his own effort all the way. A guilty thought had come into his mind: I doubt if it had not half shaped itself to him before he left the library. But, under cover of the night, we seem less afraid to entertain the sinful suggestions we harbored, hid even from ourselves, in the day. What if, in his extraordinary need, he should help himself by making use of this speech as his own? He argued with himself, as the Devil can teach a man to argue, that it would be no great wrong. He could write as well as this was written, perhaps better; with more originality of thought, and variety of illustration, if he had only his usual power: therefore in using it he should win no undue credit, only save the reputation he had already earned. He should wrong no one; for the essay had been long forgotten, and would never be recognized; and, moreover, the reputation of its author rested upon maturer works.

The thought presented a great temptation. In this way all his difficulties would be removed, his wearisome task be at an end, and his credit as a writer be uninjured. He would not take the essay just as it was, but re-arrange it, give it a new title, and introduce into it such thoughts of his own as seemed relevant.

He had grown hardened and reckless.

Present relief from a little of the intolerable weight upon his mind was all he seemed to care for. He had led Tom into sin with little compunction: it was part of his punishment that he should now yield so easily to the same temptation himself..

His mind soon made up as to his course, he set himself to making such changes in the stolen essay as should make it better suited to its pretended authorship and to the new name he had chosen for it. Such parts of that which he had already written as were best and most appropriate, more to propitiate his conscience than for any need of them, he ingeniously combined with the stolen paragraphs; pleased to see the parts matching so well in style and sentiment, that no ordinary observer could have told where the piecing was done.

By the time he had finished this work, he had so depraved his conscience, that he hardly seemed to know himself the lie he was making. He handed in the piece for his professor's examination with almost as much complacency as if it had been entirely his own. He was sure that it would be approved. He began to feel now as if he had in some measure regained freedom from care. Tom had promised to obtain the money his friend had asked for as soon as possible, and he would be as good as his word. Cyril thought he might reasonably, therefore, dismiss his anxiety about his obligation; and began to feel more confidence in his ability to make a way out of his troubles.

17

CHAPTER XIII.

ABOUT DRESS.

"Girt about with truth."

TWO weeks passed swiftly away, and the day of the Junior Exhibition was at hand. The professor of elocution had been hearing the speakers rehearse in the chapel on Saturday afternoon; and those who had finished their parts were gathered by the door, talking together, and criticising the remaining speakers. The committee of arrangements, of whom Cyril was one, were holding some discussion together, when they were addressed by a vain little fellow named Timmens. Timmens's chief inspiration all through his college course had been the thought of an opportunity of showing his grace and ability upon a public stage. Through lack of breeding, and on account of straitened circumstances, that thwarted all his desire for display, he had met countless mortifications in his career, without, however, becoming at all humbler or wiser.

He brought the question to the committee, whether the speakers at the exhibition must all wear dress-suits. "Because," he continued with eagerness, "I've been making inquiries; and I find there ain't but seven out of twenty of us that have got any 'swallow-tails.'"

"Is that so?" asked Napier, one of the committee, a youth in whose consideration an elegant toilet was almost a point of good morals. "That don't sound very well for the class, seems to me. I don't see how a fellow could wear any thing but a dress-coat on the stage. They'll have to get suits if they haven't got 'em."

"But," said Johnson, a farmer's quick-witted boy, with strong common sense, but not old enough to be entirely independent of the notions of style prevalent among those with whom he was mingling, "don't you think it's rather rough on a fellow to make him spend sixty or seventy-five dollars just to make a ten-minutes' shine with ? I'd rather have the money for something else."

" Why, it isn't just for one occasion : you always want a dress-suit, man. It's a means of civilization ; enables a man to embrace with credit all the opportunities he has of going into the best society. Keep yourself suitably dressed, and you can go anywhere."

" Yes," said another, — a minister's son, like Cyril. " But suppose you really haven't the money to pay for the means of civilization : what then ? "

" Why, then," said Napier a little scornfully, " of course I don't know what you can do. But I'd advise all of you who can, for the credit of the class, to get properly dressed. You fellows, most of you, don't go anywhere where there are ladies from one term's end to another. You think you don't need any thing but hob-nailed boots and rusty walking-suits to lounge round college in : and so, when you do happen to want something better, you think it's too much trouble or expense to get it just for this, or just for that; and you do without. It's a disgrace to you, I think.

"But then," he added, turning to one or two intimate friends who stood near him, and lowering his voice, "what a pity it is that half the fellows that get good appointments are poor fellows! On such occasions as this, we hardly make a decent show of gentlemen."

Cyril felt a twinge of shame. How was it that he was going to make a show in wearing the traditional dress of Napier's gentleman?

Meanwhile, Timmens had turned to some of those, who, like himself, suffered from the lack of black broadcloth, and was explaining to them the plan by which he thought he might satisfy his vanity in spite of his poverty; for indeed he did feel that it would be a serious mortification to be obliged to appear upon the stage in costume not the most approved.

"Here we are, fellows," he said, "with coats and pants of all shades. I say, it won't do; but I can't afford to have a new suit any more than the rest of you."

"Well, what are you going to do about it, then?" said Johnson.

"Why, I'll tell you. Subscribe and hire a suit that'll fit the average of us; and let each one take his turn to speak in it. The fit of the coat won't be noticed a little way off; and there isn't such an awful difference in our sizes anyway." And Timmens straightened himself beside tall Johnson, very much like the frog that was so sure of her ability to swell to the size of an ox.

"Well," said Johnson, smiling, "if you could make that plan answer, I should think the rest of us might. But I never wore anybody's clothes but my own yet; and I shouldn't like to be doing it for the first time in public."

"But you see," said Timmens with great earnestness, "you haven't got any clothes that are fit now; but, for half a dollar apiece, ten of us might have a suit, and come out in real stunning style. I don't see what else there is to do. They've laid down the law that we must wear black, and we can't afford to buy it. If we do the best we can in this way, nobody can complain.

"You see," continued Timmens, who was

going to make a capital pettifogger for pertinacity and ingenuity, " I don't say we shall make any pretense about it. We can have a dressing-room off that side of the stage ; and we go in there in gray or brown clothes, and come out in black ones. It's like tableaux, or any thing else, when we've got to play a part, and have a dress suited to it. Anybody may understand that takes the trouble to notice. We don't pretend any thing about it. Ain't that sensible ground to put it on ? What do you all say ? "

" I say," said Bowson, his eyes twinkling, " it's a capital idea. I go in for it. It'll save me seventy-four and a half dollars, and very likely a row with my paternal about another bill he didn't expect."

Bowson was one who had a very liberal allowance from his father, but who, having little taste for general society, and plenty of ways of spending for his own gratification other than in dress, was more frequently seen in clothing proper for the base-ball ground, or the boating-house, than in any thing more elegant. He was too much of a boy yet to care a great deal for conventionalities; and yet he, too, felt it incumbent on him, upon this occasion, to do as others of his means did.

But the considerations he had expressed were not all that influenced him. There was always in Bowson a flow of kindly sympathy toward others, revealing itself under many disguises, in hidden ways, that was like the laughing meadow-brook, along whose course flowers and fresh grasses spring up, and hide the sweet waters by which they flourish. He saw these " poor fellows," with as strong a desire to be in the fashion as other young men, gathered together to help each other put the best face possible upon their little vexation; and, while Napier deplored their condition as discreditable to the class, a generous impulse moved Bowson with good-natured hypocrisy to pretend that he was one of their party, well aware that the companionship of one not necessitated to do as they did made their case easier, and conscious that his merry humor could make pass off lightly what might be, to some of them at least, an awkward and trying matter. And when he said gayly, " A capital plan ! " there was a brightening immediately in some of the faces that had been a little anxious and discontented.

Even Johnson began to think it was no such discreditable thing to wear other people's clothes, provided it was an understood matter, and a necessary part of the evening's ceremonies.

But while they were settling the arrangement, getting the names of those who would subscribe, and agreeing to whom the coat that was to answer for all should be fitted, John Seelye came down from the long drilling in pronunciation and gesture to which the professor of elegant taste had felt it necessary to subject him.

" Halloo ! " said Timmens : " here's another ! Put your name down to our subscription, Seelye, and have a share in the dress-coat for the exhibition."

" What ? " said John, surprised.

" Why, we fellows that haven't got good clothes to speak before the ladies in, have to 'rag out' somehow for the credit of the class; and we are going to do it on the co-operation principle, — we subscribe and hire a coat, and each one wears it in turn."

" Big and little, long and short, fat and lean," said Bowson gravely.

John could not help smiling. " Do you mean, Timmens," he said, " that I am to wear the same coat as you ? "

" Why, yes," said Timmens. " It'll be a little too tight for you, and a little too loose for me ; but it won't make much difference. If there's any fellow that really can't wear it, I guess he can borrow one among the fellows."

John was still smiling; but he shook his head. " No, Timmens," said he, " I won't borrow a coat, nor hire one. If the ladies don't like the best clothes I've got, I'm sure I'm sorry ; but I can't help it."

" But you see," said Timmens, " it's customary to wear a black suit; and the committee are anxious to have all of us do so that possibly can."

" But I can't," said John. " I have not got

one; and no man's coat will fit me but my own."

"Ho!" said Bowson, trying his powers of persuasion: "you needn't feel so big! Here's Johnson, as broad-shouldered as you are: if we can fix him in it, I guess we can you. Come, now, you ain't going up there with those brown clothes: do as the rest of us do."

"Yes," said John, "I'm going up with these very clothes. I'm sorry you don't like 'em, fellows; but you see I couldn't wear any other. To dress up in fine clothes that don't belong to me, just for one occasion, seems to me a little like deceiving folks. I don't want to look better or richer than I am, even for five minutes, and to a house full of strangers. There's one lady at least, I know, would take no pleasure in seeing me so."

"Eh! who's that?" said Bowson curiously.

"My sister," said John, speaking soberly. "She taught me the first things I ever learned; and one of them was to speak and act truly in all manner of little things if I wanted to be true in great things."

There was a little silence at this earnest mention of a sister's teaching. I will say here, that, at the exhibition, the fellows saw this sister of John's. He had reserved for her a prominent seat, and waited upon her with great respect. She was a New-England school-mistress, over forty years of age, tall and angular, and very plain in face and dress; but the shrewd, bright and kindly expression of her face proved hers to be one of the characters that always distribute strength and blessing in every sphere where they work. She it was, who, with the most limited opportunities of education herself, had been wise enough to inspire her young brother with the reverence for cultivation which had brought him to college and insured his success there. There was reason why he should wait upon her with marked respect; and she had a right to be pleased and proud over the results of her work as she heard him speak.

"But you don't really think there's any thing wrong in our just putting on another coat to speak in, do you?" said Johnson to Seelye.

"Why, no," said John, considering. "I wouldn't say it was wrong; and yet it seems a little *like* wrong. You see, you are not independent enough to wear what you've got, because folks think you ought to have something else. You haven't got it, and so you contrive to *seem* to have it. And, the next time you can't do exactly as other people do, you will be still less independent, and you will contrive some way to *seem* again. And so, when you get farther on in life, and perhaps get a wife that feels just as you do, — only more so, — you will want to appear better off than you are on a great many occasions; and you'll cheat yourself out of comfort, and cheat other people with falsities, and very likely get into debt, and make a bad citizen."

"Phew — ew!" said Bowson. "And all because I changed my coat to speak at the Junior Exhibition!"

"Yes," said John, smiling; "just to please the ladies with the show. Don't you see how bad it is to encourage them in such ideas? Be sure they'll make you sorry for it one of these days. Instead of letting them lead you into unnecessary extravagance, you ought, by your example and ideas, to check their tendency that way."

" Phew — ew !"   cried Bowson   again. " You don't mean to make us responsible for all their follies ? "

" No," said John, " except as every man is, in a measure, responsible for public opinion.   I don't know much about women myself, except one good one ; but I judge they are pretty much like the rest of the world in wishing to do as others do, and are as much influenced by what they think you require as you are this minute by what you think they will consider proper.   But you needn't go out of your way to settle your duties to them : just look out for your duty to yourself.   You have a perfect right to do as you please, boys, in this little thing ; but as for me," — swinging his hat, and imitating the endeavor he had been making in his elocution-lesson, — " give me liberty in honesty, or give me death."

" Hurrah for Seelye !" cried Bowson as

John passed out. "There's the genuine invincible pluck that'll go through fire and water, silk and broadcloth, after common sense, as easy as a bullet through paper. I say, fellows, I like what he says. What do you say? Don't you think, now, we owe it as a duty to our fair sisters to show them our independence of a stupid old custom, by making our bow to them in the best clothes we've got, without going out to hire something better? It's a mean kind of shamming, after all, to wear one thing in the audience, and another thing upon the stage. It's degrading the occasion, as if it were a sort of play."

"So I say," answered Johnson heartily. "I shall do as Seelye does. I don't believe I could speak a single word if I got up there in another man's clothes, I should feel so cheap. I'd rather wear my gray coat, if folks do stare."

"It won't be any matter at all," said another, "as long as there are enough of us to keep each other in countenance."

"What do you say, Timmens?" asked

Bowson, perceiving slyly that the aspiring youth's countenance had fallen somewhat.

"Why, if the rest don't care, of course I don't," said Timmens. "But I don't believe that backwoods fellow knows any thing; and I guess you'll all be rather mortified, when it comes case in hand, not to be dressed up properly."

"Well, if we are," said Bowson, "we'll consider what we're doing, by the power of example, for all the giddy girls; and that'll console us. I guess we'll abide by what clothes we've got."

Cyril, whom Napier had left, and who stood by and listened to this discussion, couldn't join in the laughter and jokes of the light-hearted crowd as they followed Bowson sauntering away. If Cyril had had John's manliness, or if he had had Bowson's good sense in choosing the honorable course when it was pointed out to him, he would not have been to-day a man harassed by debt and dishonesty. He went away to his room, bitterly reproaching himself for his folly, but not yet remembering that the fear of the Lord, the wisdom that the weakest mind upon the smallest occasions may take for its sure defense, would have protected him if he had not cast it away.

18

CHAPTER XIV.

THE EXHIBITION.

"For he is cast into a net by his own feet."

CYRIL'S stolen oration had come back to him unsuspected, and with praises. He had perfected himself in speaking it. He felt no fear in using it: it had been forgotten for twenty years.

On that evening of the exhibition, all other anxieties were swallowed up in one. That afternoon he had received a short note from his sister, bidding him take the first train home after the speaking, for his father had grown unexpectedly and rapidly worse, and was not expected to survive more than a day or two longer. Before the warning of such an impending sorrow all other fears looked trivial, even while they added an unspeakable remorse to its weight.

Cyril was one of the ushers, and wore again the blue ribbon in his button-hole. But his manner to-night was very different from the gay complacency he had shown at the promenade concert. Not all the " nods and becks and wreathed smiles " of the young ladies of his acquaintance in various, parts of the house could call any answering smile upon his pale, wan face, or enliven the weary, absorbed manner in which he was performing his duties.

As soon as the music began, and the rustle of dresses, and stir of seating the late-comers, had subsided, he went up to the corner near the stage, where some of his classmates were, and, finding a seat among them, leaned his head upon his hand, trying to banish the thoughts which crowded so thick and fast upon his mind, that he feared they would utterly drive out the speech he had committed to memory so carefully. His companions rallied him upon his downcast looks, attributing them to the nervousness which excited some of the others who were to be speakers. So, at last, he gently told them what news he had received from home; and, after that, he could not but be touched and comforted by the kind consideration and sympathy they showed him.

One after another of his classmates appeared upon the stage, and went through with what was to each the great event of the evening; each receiving, as he finished, a hearty round of applause from his friends below. There was Johnson, whose frank address and simple good sense made up for some boyishness in his thought, and mode of expression. There was Napier, whose neat little essay, fine and smooth and finished, and fragrant with delicate flowers of fancy, was so very characteristic; there was Timmens, whose appearance at last, in a very stylish dress-suit, created almost audible laughter among some who had heard the conversation recorded in the last chapter, and whose ludicrous oration upon Daniel Webster, of whose mighty genius it was not in the nature of possibility for Timmens's little head to hold the remotest conception, completed the amusement of the hearers. There was Bowson, whose bright and humorous essay, and whose popularity, won him a double round of applause. There was John Seelye, whose words, concise, plain, and forcible, caused at least one face in the audience to beam with intense satisfaction.

But Cyril had hardly heard one word of the whole, or ceased from the mental repetition of his piece,—an occupation he found the safest to keep off agonizing thoughts. He had applauded when the rest did, as a matter of course ; and now and then the fragment of some stately sentence about truth or honor or immortality — those lofty things that so many youth love to dignify their essays by writing about, but not their lives by striving for — would catch his ear, distressing him with a sound like the loud outcry of public blame.

At last his own name was called ; and collecting himself, with the remembrance of the public eye upon him, he put his manuscript into the hand of his prompter, and went toward the stage.

He passed, as he went, a stranger sitting in one of the front pews. He was a noticeable man, with fine and intellectual features, and an exceedingly cheerful and animated expression. His bright dark eyes let nothing escape their notice, and seemed to convey to him a better understanding of men and things than most persons can gain from mere vision. Those eyes were watching the events of the evening with an interest different from the quiet, condescending one of most middle-aged persons present; with an interest as fresh and genuine as that of the most enthusiastic school-girl in the house. The stranger was reviewing the scenes of his youth for the first time after a lapse of twenty years.

His name was one never mentioned without complimentary titles, — such as the honorable, the eloquent, the wise, the accomplished; and the learned president and professors of the college, upon whom he had looked with such awe when he received his diploma at their hands, had hastened to pay him marks of respect as soon as mention was made of his presence in the town. One of those professors sat beside him now, answering his questions; a pale, stooping, grave man, whose quiet face was a complete contrast to the stranger's bright, vivacious one. The one man was like a golden lamp all aflame for light and warmth; the other like a silver censer, from which the softly-consuming ashes of precious intellectual growths — growths found dried and shut up in many books — diffused a sweet, ever-ascending perfume, an air sacred and stimulating, that youth could not breathe without refinement.

The stranger was saying to himself that no consciousness of success now was half as sweet as that with which he descended the stairs of that stage twenty years ago amidst the applause his youthful effort had excited. As he sat and watched the young men, he seemed to have returned to that hour. He was one of them, passing through just such emotions as those with which they went up and descended from the stage. None of them guessed how much sympathy was in the heart of this distinguished-looking stranger. He appeared so keen, and perhaps so critical, that some of them almost faltered as they spoke, catching his eye upon them.

Now, as Cyril went forward to the stage, his appearance especially attracted this gentleman. "There goes myself, I think," he silently soliloquized, leaning forward to look,— "my very self as I was twenty years ago. Only if my promise equaled this young man's, as I judge it from his looks, how far short of it I must have fallen!

"But then," he continued, after another glance at Cyril's face, as it now looked down from the stage, "I surely never wore a face as wearied and melancholy as that. My life was all bright and hopeful in those days. It is sad — it betokens something wrong, I am afraid — to see a brow so youthful so darkened. What can be the cause?"

And then he thought, "How gracefully he stands! What a sweet and flexible voice he has! What an elegant and striking opening sentence that is! This young man is one who has certainly all the gifts of a successful speaker; and I see, by the fire brightening in his eye, and the color coming upon his cheek, that he loves to use them.

"Ah! what is this? He is hitting upon the very vein of thought where I fancied I had found gold twenty years ago, when I won the Appleton medal. This is curious, — very curious. Hark!"

The stranger ceased his soliloquy in astonishment, listening to the words of the discourse. If any of those near had been watching his face, they would have been amazed at the startled and dismayed look it wore in the few following seconds. He could scarcely believe his ears as he heard Cyril uttering sentences as familiar, as much a part of himself as it were, as his own name, — sentences, every word of which had been a carefully-placed touch that helped to make pictures, all of whose brightness no eye but the author's could ever see. Himself as he had been he had called Cyril; but was there any possible likeness of mind that could enable one man to think the very same thoughts, and express them in the very same words, as another? Ah, no! As the gentleman began to see the truth through the bewilderment into which he had been at first thrown, his heart sank with shame and pity for poor Cyril. He knew he could not be mistaken: the words of his most earnest and ambitious youthful effort were like none he had written since. Moreover, they were coming, in their carefully-made arrangement and connection, back to his mind, anticipated from Cyril's lips.

The stranger was not angry, but a little hurt at feeling that what had once seemed, even though at so distant a day, sacred and noble, the best fruit of his mind, should be stolen and profaned. The most like to an unkind emotion that he had, he experienced in the sarcastic scorn which curled his lip as he listened when his first astonishment had subsided.

"You do it well," he began silently commenting again. "You evidently understand it. Who could suspect you had stolen what you repeat with such earnestness? *That* accent I know I did not use in that place;

but, nevertheless, your way renders the meaning with considerable power. Ah! you have changed that illustration for one which alludes to things of more modern occurrence. Cunningly done ; and those interpolations come as if they belonged there. Ah, what a pity that such fine talent should employ itself in fraud ! "

And, with that sigh, all lighter and more unworthy feeling vanished from the noble heart in kind concern for the poor youth who stood there, so unconscious of his disgrace ; nay, so proud because the audience were remarkably attentive to the words they deemed his own.

" What shall I do ? " thought the stranger. " To let him go unaware of his detection would be most cruel kindness. Shall I go and talk with him myself, but let the thing be for ever hidden between himself and me ? But I am afraid that will not answer. One who could do such a thing as this must require bitter and long-to-be-remembered punishment. Besides, he has deceived the whole community. He has cheated his teachers, and entered into rivalry with his companions unfairly. They have all a right to know."

And so he thought it best to make the revelation while he had the proof ready to hand. He touched the arm of the professor beside him, who was listening with unusual pleasure. The change in the stranger's face, which, lately animated and smiling, was now grave and severe, surprised the old man; but how he was shocked when he listened to what the stranger had to tell! He could hardly bring himself to believe it.

"Sir," he said, very much agitated, "this is such a serious charge to bring against the young man! There must be some mistake, — some remarkable coincidence: it can not be a fraud."

"Listen," said the stranger; and he began anticipating Cyril's sentences, word for word, for whole paragraphs; while the professor, listening with astonishment and grief, was no longer able to doubt Cyril's guilt. The real author of the main part of the speech readily distinguished such portions of it as were not his own, bidding the old man notice a certain difference in Cyril's manner of delivering them; an intensity and weight being given to that which he had himself written, which no art could teach him to use in.reciting the compositions of another, as an additional proof. Cyril's deed was but too evident: not even the charity that hopeth all things could refuse to see it.

As Cyril finished his speech, and made his parting bow, his glance distinguished two out of the thousand faces of the audience, — two that were looking at him with such severity and sorrow, that he was startled. He left the stage with an uneasy feeling, that the shower of bouquets he was forced to stop and gather up, and the triple round of applause that was given him, could not soothe away.

Those two faces were still turned upon him when he had come down and stood receiving the congratulations of his classmates. They troubled him exceedingly. They seemed to make visible to him the aspect of his conscience, against whose vexation he had so persistently shut the door of his heart. He could not stay to endure them longer. He began hastily taking leave of his friends, explaining that he must prepare to start for home immediately.

They let him go with many expressions of affection and sympathy. At the door, he found Tom Raddon waiting for him. Cyril was glad of an opportunity to speak with him. He put his arm through Tom's, and asked him to come a little way down the street. Tom was to remain in town during the short spring vacation. Cyril spoke of his father's sickness, and of his being obliged to hurry away, leaving many of his affairs in disorder. He asked if Tom would send on to him any letters, especially city letters, that might come to his address here in his absence ; and, if at any time Tom should get the sixty dollars he had promised, would he put it in a directed envelope which Cyril gave him, and have it sent to its destination ? The envelope was addressed to the melodeon merchant, and contained his bill. Cyril briefly explained the story to Tom, as he must needs do.

"I paid for my clothes first, you see," he

said, "because that had been longest owed.
And now I have to look to you, Tom, for the
other. It's a worse debt, I know; for I'm responsible to those who have once raised the
money to pay it."

Cyril could see that even Tom was somewhat shocked at the revelation. "I was a
fool, Tom," he said; "but, oh! I've suffered
for it, I tell you: so forgive me, and stand
by me, won't you? for I've no one else to
look to."

Tom's generous heart was easily softened.
He promised to do all for Cyril that lay in his
power, and assured him that it should be all
made right soon.

Cyril thanked him with sincere gratitude;
and, at the door of his room, they shook hands
and parted.

Cyril had hardly left the exhibition-hall,
when Prof. Reeve, and the gentleman sitting
with him, after a short consultation together,
rose, and departed also. They followed Cyril
and Tom; so that, when the latter turned back,
he met them only a few rods off. He hardly

noticed the circumstance, though; for he was hurrying to get back before the exhibition closed. There was a certain young lady there, with her mother, for whom he had taken great pains in securing the best seats in the house, and whom he would not, for any thing less than his friendship for Cyril, have lost the pleasure of escorting home. Tom's partiality for Miss Owens, his companions said, was ceasing to be a subject for jokes. When a fellow grew restless every night in the week that he could not meet a certain young lady, yet was held back, by a dread of intruding, to let long intervals pass between his visits to her; when, after each one, he grew strangely quiet, gentle, and reserved; when he never spoke her name any more in careless intercourse among his comrades; when it evidently made him tremble to think he had dared offer her an invitation, and he feared the very choicest seat in the house was not good enough for her,—why, then the matter was beginning to look serious. And the fellows shook their heads while they sagely opined that it was a sad thing for Tom to fall so much in love in that quarter; that such a rough uncivilized fellow as he would only be ruthlessly scorned by one who was the very flower of culture and refinement.

19

CHAPTER XV.

THE DOUBLE LOSS.

"He hath destroyed me on every side, and I am gone; and mine hope hath He removed like a tree."

CYRIL was in his room, glad, oh! so glad, that the evening was over, and that he might hurry home. He had changed his suit for other clothes, — that hateful suit, that he never wished to wear again. He could not take it home, but would leave it here, with orders, if he did not come back to college, to have it sold with some other little possessions, the value of which might help pay his debt to the Sunday school. He was hastily packing the rest of his clothing and some of his books, when a knock upon his door interrupted him. Judge how he was startled, when he opened it, to meet the two severe and sad faces, a passing glimpse of which had so disturbed him as he left the stage a half-hour since!

Cyril stood speechless with surprise and vague fear. He could not summon enough presence of mind to make any respectful salutation to his professor, or to ask them to walk in.

"Mr. Rivers," said the professor, "we have a few minutes' business with you."

Cyril held the door a little wider open : he had not yet recovered the use of his voice.

"This," said the professor as they entered, motioning toward the stranger, and fixing his serious eyes upon Cyril's face, "is the Hon. Mr. Elton of Leroy."

Every other fear had entered Cyril's mind as he looked at his visitors ; but the detection of his essay—for some curious reason, probably because he had, from the beginning, felt so safe in the fraud—he had forgotten. At the mention of this name, then, he was completely overwhelmed. The entire suddenness of the blow took from him all power of dissimulation. He could not hide his consternation. His face grew deadly white ; and he staggered, so that the stranger, full of pity, reached out a hand to support him. "Mr. Rivers," he said as he drew him to a chair, "I see you know why we have come."

But Cyril, still scarcely overcoming the faintness that had fallen upon him, with the first return of thought made an instinctive effort to conceal his desperate shame.

"I — I do not, sir," he answered. "Have you a telegram from my father, professor ?"

"Your father, sir ? " said the professor angrily, and yet puzzled by the apparent earnestness and good faith of the question.

"He is very sick," said Cyril. "He is dying, they say. I only heard to-day. I am preparing to go to him. I feared, when I saw you, you might have come to break to me worse news from him. That was why I was so overcome."

The quickness and adroitness of this feint puzzled the professor still more, and astonished Mr. Elton ; but he was not in the least deceived.

"Young man," he said, fixing his stern, bright eyes upon Cyril, "you are telling a falsehood. You know why we came, and why you trembled to see us."

Cyril shrank cowering under the glance.

"Mr. Rivers," said the professor, "we have come from the exhibition-hall, where we listened to your recitation of an essay which this gentleman recognized as one written by himself twenty years ago. He proved the theft to me by anticipating the very words as they came from your mouth. I have brought this charge to you to ask if there is any thing you have to urge in its extenuation."

"It is a mistake, sir," said Cyril, his face burning now with shame. "I did find a speech in the library, following the same train of thought as mine, and did quote a few paragraphs from it; but mine was almost finished before I came across Mr. Elton's, sir."

"Where is your manuscript?" asked the professor.

It was near at hand: but Cyril could not give it up; it was only another proof of his guilt. He seemed hemmed in on every side. In his desperation, his head drooped again; and conviction wrote itself in every line of his face.

Then Mr. Elton spoke to him again more kindly, but plainly.

" Mr. Rivers," he said, " you hesitate to give it up because it will falsify your statement. But there are three — you and I, and the One who knows all hearts — who do not need its testimony. To have the condemnation of God and your own soul, that is the most terrible thing. Of what consequence is it, since you have that, whether the reprobation of 'the world is added? Why are you so afraid of it, and not of continuing to deceive? You must have gone far in the habit before you could come to this. You surely want now to turn back : you ought to find comfort in the thought of standing entirely undisguised in the sight of all men. Just blame and just contempt ought to be sweet to you, if, bowed down under them, you may once more draw the breath of an honest man. Don't, I beseech you, try to hide behind a barrier of lies any more: come manfully and take your punishment, and be taught by it. Some time, you will call this a fortunate hour, — this hour of bitter disgrace. I believe it is the most fortunate hour you have seen these many years. I hope, that, in the good providence of God, it is meant to save you from terror and despair in that awful time when the secrets of *all* hearts must be revealed, and when many for shame will call upon the rocks to fall upon them and hide them. Surely, surely, you would not, if you could, go on with all this sin hidden and unrebuked till then."

Those were words spoke in season, — words that reached Cyril's reason and moral sense, and led him out of the confusion and darkness with which his mind was overwhelmed. He was silent a few moments: and then he hastily seized his manuscript essay, that lay under some papers upon the table; and, reaching from a shelf the printed copy of Mr. Elton's oration, he put them into the professor's hand.

"Sir," he said with white lips and trembling

voice, " there are the proofs of my guilt, if you want any other than what you have heard. I copied the oration almost *verbatim*, with very slight additions and alterations."

The professor took the papers; and, his indignation disarmed by this confession, he could almost have shed tears for grief and compassion.

" Mr. Rivers," he said, " I can not express my sorrow and surprise at what you have done. It is my duty to lay these papers before the faculty; and probably, in simple justice to your classmates and the public, the story will be made known to them also. But you have heretofore borne a good character, and you have many friends here. Is there nothing I can state to extenuate your deed? Was there any extraordinary temptation which should be mentioned with the sin?"

" No," answered Cyril, much agitated, — " nothing that furnished me the shadow of an excuse. I could not write as easily as usual; and then this pamphlet came in my way, and I used it without a scruple. That was all."

There was a sorrowful silence in the room. The professor at last rose to go. " We will not keep you from going to your father," he said. " The action of the faculty in this matter will be communicated to you."

But the stranger extended his hand to Cyril as he went. " Our first meeting," he said, " has been a painful one ; but surely, by God's blessing, I shall find when I meet you again, whether in this world or the next, that its result has been joyful. Only turn to your Father in repentance, and ask him to make it so. That will save you so much suffering ! "

They left Cyril too much overcome by the suddenness of the blow to realize all that had occurred. He felt no such acute mortification as might have been expected ; for he seemed half stunned. He could think only vaguely : a sense of unreality dulled his emotions. He understood that all was gone now that he had enjoyed and hoped and acted for here at college ; but he seemed to find himself resigned to that, as one wearied out in struggling is glad to be forced to sink down when strength fails.

He kept whispering to himself, with a levity that was almost like that by which an insane person will show his uneasy misery, " It is all over with me! ah, well, it is all over with me ! "

He felt only anxious to get away. He hurried his things into his portmanteau, and hastened off as if for his life, haunted by the feeling that he fled to hide himself from a storm of reprobation that followed fast after him.

He hurried down to the dark dépôt, confused and dreary, and it seemed ominous of such places as all the rest of his clouded existence must be spent in. He even likened the darkness and the smoke and din, and the hard-faced, hurrying, selfish men that pushed by him, to the atmosphere and the companions he might find in that awful world for which he thought he had been deliberately trying to make his character fit.

As he entered the train, two of his classmates, going the same road for a distance, hailed him, delighted at the prospect of his companionship ; but he shrank away from them as though they and he could by no means come together as companions any more. He could not realize that they had not yet learned all, he seemed to himself so thoroughly exposed and condemned. He passed to a remote corner of the train without answering them a word.

As the train rushed on through the night, Cyril's mind ran faster among gloomy thoughts. A feeling of the strangeness of his situation impressed him. How wonderfully soon he had become accustomed to disgrace! He seemed to have borne it all his life instead of a few short hours. And yet how new the story would be to others! — to Tom, to the class-mates who had so lately called him an honor to their number, to Miss Kerlie, and all the gay friends who had smiled admiration upon him only this evening. It seemed impossible that he could be the same brilliant and favored Cyril Rivers they had known, — he who seemed now to be old in wretchedness, to have lived long ashamed and confounded, to have borne always a name that was a by-word and a reproach. And yet the change had befallen only a few short hours ago.

And then the stranger had called it " *a fortunate hour* " that took him from that brilliant life to this. How strange that was ! Cyril had seemed to believe the word when it was spoken. How could that have been ? If he could only understand the thought again ! " A fortunate hour " ! How the words puzzled him ! He had had ingenuity enough once to understand paradoxes ; but this seemed to escape his comprehension, he was now so dull and bewildered.

And then he fell to wondering if, with his old reputation, his old power had gone too, — the intellect he once possessed ; if he was to be always the confused, cowed creature he was now, and should never again be able to find either talent or acquirement to help him climb back to rank with other men. How strange and how ominous was that loss of ability which had tempted him to copy Mr. Elton's speech ! The thought of it now filled him with despair. He remembered, when he read that fatal essay, he had called himself the equal in intellect of its writer. Ah, what a vain boast it was ! He knew better now. Cyril Rivers, this poor fool taken in his own folly, could never be a man like that, — never, never! — a man so noble and successful; a man whose riches of wisdom, and fullness of life, overflowed in gifts of blessing wherever he went.

Yet this man had not looked upon Cyril with utter scorn: he had spoken kindly and hopefully, and he had called that "a fortunate hour." Ah! Cyril thought if he could only catch the clew to the meaning of those words!

With such vague, wandering thoughts, Cyril struggled through the three hours of his night-journey; rousing himself, as if waking from a dull nightmare, when the train reached the station. The walk through the town to his house still further dispelled the bewilderment into which he had fallen: and, as he neared home, he forgot the new aspect life wore to him; forgot the new character he bore in the world, to whose strangeness he was trying to submit himself; and remembered nothing but his father's state. A torturing anxiety urged on his steps.

Dark as it still was, he saw the door open as he drew near the house, as though anxious eyes had been watching for him. His sister came down to the gate to meet him. "O Cyril!" she said, " we are so glad you've come! We wanted to send for you before ; but he would not let us, though we feared he might not live to see you. O Cyril! he is dying!—father is dying! "

Her cry had a pleading tone, as though she begged for her brother's help in a trouble so awful ; but he could not answer her even by taking her hand in his own.

He followed her into the house. Some of his father's parishioners were there, talking together in low tones, anxious to be of service to the family of their beloved minister. One and another reached out a hand of sympathy to Cyril as he passed among them ; and they were full of compassion when they saw his altered looks. Alas! that kind feeling toward the young man was changed to indignation by the close of another day.

Cyril was led directly to the chamber of the

dying man. There lay the father who had labored his life away for his children ; whose faithful love had never failed to find a way to grant his son every reasonable wish, every needful good ; who had loved him too much, perhaps, — set his hopes too fondly upon the boy's promise and success.

It appeared that he would not live to see those hopes cast down. His eye was dim, and his face sunken ; yet it brightened when he turned it toward his son's : and his wasted hands had yet strength to move themselves to meet Cyril's grasp. " My son, my dear son ! " he cried fondly.

And, at those words, a flood of love and sorrow swelled in Cyril's soul, and swept away its darkness and confusion. He saw the truth concerning his sin. He forgot the hush in the chamber of death, — every thing but the longing for forgiveness before his father should go hence to return never more. He fell upon his knees by the bedside, crying in anguish, " O father ! I can not be called your son : I am not worthy. I have sinned against you. O father, father ! "

The cry ended in terrible weeping; so violent, that, in alarm for the dying man, Cyril's mother tried to lead him away. But his father motioned her back. The peace in which he had put off all cares, and had lain waiting for death during these last few hours, was not to be broken. He was too far withdrawn from the world for any of its agitations to shake him now. But his fatherly love was still unfailing. He roused himself from the lethargy of death once more, to offer help in his child's need.

"What is it, my child?" he asked.

"O father! it is too late to tell it all now; but I have done so wrong!"

"But there's the atonement, my child. Whatever you have done, there is the atonement. I am thinking of that." And then his voice sank to a whisper, and he seemed talking to himself. "He will suffer," he said: "we must all suffer when we have sinned. But that is nothing if we are saved from the sin at last, — nothing, nothing. When we have washed our robes, and made them white in the blood of the Lamb, we shall *come out* of great tribulation into perfect peace."

He fell into insensibility; while Cyril, repressing his sobs, fixed his gaze upon his father's face, and held his hand, as if comfort and wisdom were dying with him. The morning had hardly dawned when the good man passed away. In the same night, Cyril was bereft of his good name and made fatherless.

20

CHAPTER XVI.

THE FALLEN TREE.

"Upright men shall be astonished at this, and the innocent shall stir up himself against the hypocrite."

THERE was wonder and regret throughout Eaton that day. At every breakfast-table, the first reader of the morning paper broke his silent perusal with an exclamation of surprise, and startled the whole family with the news one short, grave paragraph contained. You guess what that news was. A consultation among the various members of the faculty at the close of the exhibition had resulted in sending to the office of the morning journal this statement, signed by the president: —

"It is my duty to inform the public that the essay spoken by Cyril E. Rivers at the junior exhibition, this evening, was not his own.

With the exception of some trifling additions and alterations, it was stolen by Mr. Rivers from the printed copy of an oration spoken by Mr. Edward Elton, during his senior year in college, twenty years ago. The speech was at once recognized by him, and the fraud has since been confessed. Since it was committed upon the public, it is our painful duty to make the discovery public also."

Imagine how this story came to Cyril's many friends. There was no refusing to believe it, since it came over the *president's honored name.* Miss Kerlie and all the gay companions of many happy hours read it, and were exceedingly shocked and grieved. The superintendent and teachers of the Sunday school read it with the utmost consternation. When they met, they looked at each other in a kind of terror, and spoke of what had happened in a low, frightened tone. Who could tell the mischief, they thought, if the scholars who had trusted and loved Cyril so much should learn the story? They were old enough to read the daily news: it could scarcely help coming to their knowledge. Who, again, could make them believe that truth and goodness really existed, when they had been once so deceived? In Cyril's class, the story, as it became known, produced a profound sensation. A portion of his disgrace seemed to rest upon all. Well might it be so with some who had laughed with him over lesser frauds. It was right that they should suffer in his punishment. But ashamed and grieved as they were, strange to say, even among those best acquainted with Cyril's character and ways, the general expression was of wonder. "How *could* he do it?" was the constantly-repeated exclamation. "How *dared* he do a thing so bold, to take such a risk for so small a gain, and when he must have foreseen how fatal would be the consequences in case of discovery? How could he have been so unwise?" Those who were best acquainted with what had gone before could not understand the riddle of his folly. They could not connect consequences with causes, and see that petty deceiving, though sanctioned by general usage, nevertheless had destroyed the moral sense of one who practiced it, till he had fallen into greater sin, and greater risk of punishment and disgrace, without knowing his position. Vanity is never wise nor scrupulous. There is no need to search for weighty and desperate motives for the rash deeds of one leading a life away from God. A little temptation will draw such a one into great and dangerous sin, while his eyes seem blinded to its greatness and its danger.

But, where all were sorrow-stricken, there was one who seemed well-nigh heart-broken over Cyril's downfall. It was Tom Raddon, who all that day sat in his room in grief that refused to be comforted. He had, of late, learned so much of Cyril, that he could not feel the surprise that others expressed; but, in deep dejection, he groaned aloud for sorrow and remorse. Sometimes he would insanely defend Cyril, vowing the whole thing to have no more foundation than in the suspicions of the malicious professors; sometimes he would desperately try to whiten his sin, alleging that many others had done things as bad, and no outcry been made; or showing how Cyril had been distracted by troubles; bringing to excuse him the very argument Cyril had used for himself. Then he would begin upbraiding himself for having urged his friend into wrong practices; for having been selfish, never helpful and kind, careful to try and keep his friend out of trouble, — a self-reproach that those who heard it, and who knew the character and the former relations of the two, were amazed to think that it should ever have suggested itself to Tom's mind. But though he had, at first, looked up to Cyril, and depended much upon him, of late they seemed to have changed places somewhat. Cyril had been downcast and dejected, and had been forced to ask for the help that Tom could give; while he had been trying to learn to depend upon himself, when Cyril used to assist him. And, no matter how grateful a man's disposition may be, he can not love those from whom he receives as tenderly as those to whom he gives. Tom was grieved for Cyril as an older brother would have been; and his grief revealed to

him his share of the responsibility of Cyril's
sin. The shock, too, with which he heard told
of another the same thing which he had himself done, opened to him a new view of his own
wickedness and unworthiness before God and
man. He was as angry with himself as grieved
for Cyril. He declared that he ought to
stand in Cyril's place, bear the same punishment, the same reproaches, the same disgrace.
But in all such talk there was no comfort, only
the more grief. He could not throw off the
discontent and remorse that possessed him.
He paced up and down, groaning at the bitterness of the thoughts in his mind, and finding
no relief anywhere.

But what he suffered to-day for Cyril was
to be augmented to-morrow. This morning's
sensation was not the only one the name and
conduct of Cyril Rivers was to make in Eaton.

Among the readers who saw that fatal
paragraph in the morning paper was the melodeon manufacturer. He read it with some
little curiosity at first, but without any emotion.
It did not surprise him; for he regarded

students generally with disgust. He considered them as some species of imperfectly-tamed wild beast, brought to mind occasionally as a mischievous nuisance, when there was a riot of their making in the streets, or he heard some story of gas-lamps broken, and gates carried off in their wanton sport. This account of Cyril's fraud matched very well with what he was always hearing of them. That was his only mental comment, until he looked once more at the name, perhaps with some cautious idea of storing it away in his remembrance.

It had a curiously familiar sound. " Cyril Rivers," he read. " Where have I heard that name before ? It can't be that I've got that name on my books. Now I think of it, who was it bought that melodeon for the Bethel Sunday School ? He certainly gave a name something like that ; but, of course, it can not be the same. Such men are not generally connected with Sunday schools."

But Mr. Harmoner got straight up from his breakfast-table, and went to the shop to turn over his books in search of that name. He

THE MELODEON MERCHANT.

came upon it with a feeling of indignation and fear. There it stood, just as in the paper,— Cyril E. Rivers; and the address that followed made it certain that it was the name of a student.

"Now," Mr. Harmoner anxiously thought, "I'll be bound, there's an imposition here. The Sunday school! A likely story they'd send a man like that to do their business for 'em. At any rate, with only that name for security, I've got no security at all. Here's something I must look into this very morning."

As speedily as possible, he wrote out his bill, and proceeded in search of his suspicious debtor. His alarm began to grow serious when Cyril's landlady informed him that her boarder had left for home the evening before.

Mr. Harmoner at once proceeded in search of the superintendent, Mr. Keep.

Mr. Keep was sorrowfully thinking of Cyril; thinking, now that the blind leader had fallen into the ditch, what he should do for the followers; how he should repair the injury to those poor, ignorant, sorely-tempted lads, who had begun to believe in right, because one they loved and trusted seemed to believe. Perhaps the story might not reach them ; but, if it did, how could it be set before them as subject for sorrow and warning, instead of an incitement to unbelief and scoffing ? While he was thinking of these things, Mr. Harmoner came in search of him.

" I believe, sir," he said, as Mr. Keep asked him to be seated, " that you are the superintendent of the Bethel-mission School."

" Yes, sir," said Mr. Keep.

" Was there a Mr. Rivers connected with your school, whose name I see in the paper to-day as that of a dishonest man ? "

" There was," said Mr. Keep. " We were, among others, deceived by his apparently fair character."

" Well, sir," said Mr. Harmoner, " perhaps I need not have been troubled ; but, you see, he purchased a melodeon from our place for the school, and I've only his name for security. I thought, after what I learned about him to-day, that I would just like to speak with some of the rest of you about the bill. Not that I feel at all uneasy at having trusted the school; but I should like to feel that the responsibility was not entirely his."

Imagine Mr. Keep's sorrow as he gathered the meaning of this! "Sir," he said, "do you mean to say that Mr. Rivers did not pay you for that melodeon?"

"He did not," said the merchant. "He said the school had some little difficulty in raising the money; but that three or four weeks would enable them to make payment. I had, of course, no distrust in letting him have the instrument."

"But the money was in his hands," said Mr. Keep. "It is a rule of ours never to go in debt for any such extra expense."

"Then," said the merchant angrily, "the scamp has stolen it! I never saw a penny of it."

Mr. Keep, dismayed at this new development, tried to allay the merchant's alarm for his debt by promising to bring the matter before the other officers of the school, and either to have the instrument returned, or the money raised to pay for it the second time. The school, he thought, would have to be responsible for the fraud of its officer; and that it should hold property unpaid for was contrary to one of the main articles of its constitution.

He earnestly begged the man not to let the matter become public; but his injunctions were little regarded. Cyril Rivers was nothing to Mr. Harmoner; and he was indignant, and, besides, had the important feeling of possessing a new development to relate of the story which was the topic of the day throughout the town. He did not anticipate that there could be any harm in telling, in a confidential way, that which occupied his mind, to the next friend he met upon the street. It was eagerly listened to, and quickly repeated. Alas! how strange is the interest with which a story of weakness and sin is heard and started!—not the sorrowful and sympathetic interest, but the curious, the amused, the scoffing interest. How rarely found, even among Christians, is the man who will refrain from taking up a reproach against his neighbor!

The story had not gone through three narrations before it came as a rich prize into the hands of the item gatherer for the local paper, and was by him rapidly put into shape for the public edification.

The next morning journal contained, therefore, a conspicuous paragraph, headed, " Further Developments: the student Cyril E. Rivers a swindler as well as a plagiarist." And then was narrated, with many a moral comment and sage reflection, Cyril's apparently cool theft from the Sunday school, of course without any of those palliations of the sin, if charity may call them palliations, of which I have told you. The nine-days' wonder had developed a new phase, and taken a new lease of life; and, if there is always a satisfaction in the discovery of delinquency, how much more when it is delinquency in high places, in the church and Sunday school, in the most refined social circle, in a minister's son, or a professor's promising *protégé!* Even in hearts naturally benevolent, how fast the first feeling of pain and surprise excited by such a story will wear off in the satisfaction of abundant food for gossip!

But we quickly become used to new events. Before the close of that day even, most of those who knew Cyril had become accustomed to his downfall. It was to them almost like a fact expected. The shadow that had fallen upon him seemed to stretch backward over all the years of their acquaintance with him; so that they seemed never to have known him as any thing but weak, vain, and deceitful. The tree once down, we soon become accustomed to contemplate it as fallen, — fit only to be removed for the burning. We soon forget to compare it sorrowfully with the one that lately towered upright in the sunshine, the glory of the garden. We walk about it as it lies prone, and examine the hidden decay that has laid it low; mark how rudely its roots have been broken from their hold, and have torn up the earth that nourished them; notice the strength of the great limbs that are crushed and broken; and coolly watch the fresh green leaves of youth and spring-time that were so beautiful high in the sunshine, withering away in the dust. It is a pity that the tree fell; but, since we can not set it up again for admiration, take it away, and let us seek another to put in its place. The shock is over now, and there is neither time nor thought to spare in long regrets.

All who really loved Cyril were doubly wounded by this second story, so unnecessarily made public. The superintendent would have given worlds if he could have kept the matter hushed, for Cyril's sake as well as the school's. Wherever he went, he was overwhelmed with questions as to the truth. His regret and mortification were unspeakable.

As for Tom, I must begin another chapter to tell you about him.

CHAPTER XVII.

TOM'S GRIEF AND HIS COMFORT.

"So Jonathan arose, in fierce anger; for he was grieved for David."

"But God is the judge: he putteth down one and setteth up another."

"Hold thou me up, and I shall be safe."

I TOLD you how Tom spent the day in his room, groaning with alternate sorrow and remorse; as restless in this trouble, which no outlay of money could smooth away, as a wounded lion.

But when, the next morning, this second part of the story came to his ears, he astonished his companions with a show of anger and distress for which they could not, for some time, discover any sufficient cause. He stormed at the Sunday-school managers and the melodeon merchant, calling them liars and defamers; asserting that there was not one word of truth in the story, and that he had authority for declaring it. Then he railed at himself, crying with angry tones that he had been a careless, ungrateful friend, fit to have no man's honor trusted to his care again; cursing himself for his forgetfulness; saying, that he might have foreseen all this yesterday, and that, if he had only had a little sense, he might have saved it all to his poor friend.

His companions, utterly confounded at his almost tragic grief, began to understand, at last, that Cyril must have left the debt that never should have been incurred, in Tom's care; for he vowed that he would make it right now at any rate, and that somebody should pay for this wanton defamation of Cyril's character. "Because a fellow had copied part of his essay from an old musty paper," thus raved Tom, "need he be charged with every other crime in the decalogue also?"

With that, he seized his hat, declaring that he would go and call John Seelye to account.

"He belonged to the Sunday school, and he had taken Cyril over there," Tom said; "and if he had had the least friendly feeling, he would have prevented this story from getting abroad."

Tom strode away with a fierce scowl upon his brow, but with his head hanging, and eyes downcast, — a man thoroughly mortified, and though defiant, yet ashamed to meet the world, before which he, quite as much as Cyril, seemed to have been publicly disgraced.

But the walk in the open air quieted his excitement; and he soon began to view things more sanely. He did not, as his friends had feared he would, break in upon John Seelye with violent invective and reproach, but appeared at the door of his room in a humble and reasonable mood.

Finding that John knew no more than he how the story had become public, he was still further mollified. He explained to John what he knew of the transaction; how Cyril had told him, that, pressed by debt, he had taken the Sunday-school money, hoping indefinitely to find some way out of the trouble before the merchant should urge his obligation; and how, when Cyril was obliged to go away, he had intrusted the whole matter to his, Tom's, friendship. And then Tom added, with many self-reproaches, that, when he might have reflected yesterday morning that one story would quickly start the other, he had taken no measure to prevent it, as he should have done.

But now Tom was going to pay the debt at any risk or inconvenience; and he wanted it made known as publicly as the fraud had been, that Cyril did not appropriate the money with any intention to cheat. Almost his last care had been to secure its payment; and his trouble about it had been one cause, no doubt, of his failure to write his essay.

As Tom told this story, he saw that John readily comprehended it, and seized as eagerly upon what small excuse there was in it for Cyril as did Tom himself. He found this man, so strict in his zeal for honesty, not, as he had fancied, full of severity for Cyril, and ready to deepen his disgrace, but as much grieved for him as was Tom's own heart ; perhaps even more deeply grieved, because John was better able to estimate the calamity of the loss of principle and reputation. He showed a heart full of sympathy both for Cyril and for Tom ; a heart that Tom perceived might be relied on for counsel and kindness in this the sorest trouble of his life.

John went with him to the superintendent to repeat the story, and to secure that it should be published as an explanation by Mr. Keep, in such form as should be most just to Cyril ; the statement being added, that his debt to the school was already discharged : for Tom was determined to pay for the melodeon that very day, if, as he said, he sold all his furniture and wardrobe. No doubt, he could have raised the money in some other way ; but he did not want the debt put off with borrowed means any more : and there was a sort of satisfaction to him in stripping his room of some of its superfluities for Cyril's sake, — of the costly clock that adorned the mantel-piece, the patent study-chair he never used, and the heavily-framed pictures, of questionable taste, that, he said, were so tiresome, always staring at him. But when he had disposed of them, and paid over the money, with severe reproaches, to the merchant, for the needless harm he had done, and when he had carried with his own hands to the newspaper office the note Mr. Keep had written to set Cyril's conduct in a more favorable light, he was still unsatisfied. Restless, he bent his steps back to John's room. Sitting there, he told him how he had done all he could think of for Cyril. "But," said he, leaning his head upon his hands with a weary sigh, "it's all of very little use."

And after a few moments he gave an uneasy jerk upon his chair, and broke forth again: "I've been about to-day, and nobody called me a liar and a cheat, or turned away from me, as if I was not fit to be spoken to, the way they would treat Rivers, to judge from their talk about him. And I say," his voice rising angrily, "that it's unjust! I have done things as wicked and mean and underhanded as ever he did. If he sold lies — as — as *she* said, I bought and used 'em. I've cheated ten times where he has once, and never winced, or troubled myself about it afterwards. Nobody puts me in the newspapers; but I say I deserve the same as he ! "

" I believe it," said John, not reproachfully, but sadly and earnestly.

The answer rather startled Tom, it was so different from any response the same complaints had brought from other men ; but it satisfied him better than any other could have done. He was longing to take his place in the light of truth.

" But they do not give me the same," he complained. " They do not publish me. The fellows do not get out of my way as if I was a pickpocket, or believe that I could steal children's money ! And if I should go to the faculty, and make a confession, they'd shut the punishment off me, just because I had confessed. And there are others, too : if they haven't gone quite so far as Rivers, they've gone the same way, and taught him to think little of the things that helped him do this. I don't want them to have the like punishment, and I'm not saying I want it myself: I couldn't bear it. I don't see how poor Rivers will. Only I don't see how it's just, that he should be the one to take it for us all. His doing was partly caused by ours, and why should he have all the penalty? If the rest of us go free, why not he, too? It's hard: I say, it's hard!"

And Tom covering his face with his hands, tears of vexation stole through his fingers.

John looked at him, and was moved with compassionating wonder at his blindness of mind. His eyes kindled, and his expression grew doubly earnest.

"Raddon," said he slowly, "do you believe in Almighty God?"

The question, and the tone in which it was put, struck impressively upon Tom's mind. He raised his head, and looked at John with solemnity and humility in his expression.

"Yes, I do," he answered. Not his early associations with paganism, not the ignorance in which his conscience had been left, not even familiarity with sin and habitual indulgence therein, could kill the faith implanted in his heart in an Almighty God, — a faith degenerated now almost into superstition, but ready, let us hope, to rise again some time to religion.

"Then," said John, "just believe it is he who is dealing with your life, and Rivers's, and the lives of every one of us. Do not sit down and chafe yourself because what you call an unlucky fortune has distributed an uneven reward. Do not suppose that you and he and the rest went on sinning unheeded, some more and some less (God only can tell which), till one of you, by an untoward chance only, pulled down upon himself the punishment you all might claim. Who sent that man here to discover Rivers just on that night, of all others in the world? Who kept you from covering that fraud about the melodeon till it was too late? I say it was God's will, and not a chance. And you are not to call it hard or unjust, either," continued John. "Do you think God loved him any the less because he interfered to stop him in such a course? We get only the warning from the fall; but, because he was suddenly laid hold upon with a heavy hand, we are not to say that we are treated more kindly than he. I tell you, God is taking care of him, rescuing him from his weakness in the best and surest possible way. And, if hard measures were necessary, you are not to complain of them, however you may be sorry, but just to believe that they are all right and kind. You are not to excuse Rivers's guilt to yourself or to him either. Offer him as much sympathy and help as you can, but not a word of exculpation. It will be a perilous thing for you both if you do.

"And another thing," continued John; "don't you lose the lesson God sends to you in his punishment, while you are complaining that you do not share it as much as you deserve. See here! Raddon, if you will learn that, so as to be all your life the better for it, you seem to lighten Rivers's guilt, to make him before all the world an instrument of good to you, instead of harm; and, besides, you will redeem the injury you and he have done each other by doing good to other men."

John spoke with enthusiasm.

"But how can I learn the lesson?" cried Tom, excited by his words. "I tell you, to go up hill is impossible for me. I've told no man till now; but I've tried these three months to get a little nearer to being an honest man, and I make nothing of it but failure. I hate myself. I don't see why I was born such a miserable dog. It's as bad with others, too, for all that I can see. Nobody can make any thing of himself but to be just as good or as bad as he was born. How can I be better? It isn't in me?"

"No," said John earnestly; "but it is in the grace of God for you. You said you believed in God, and, by his works, you must know he is a kind God. Do you suppose, then, he would let you come into the world, inheriting so much weakness and wickedness in your character, and then just leave you alone to manage with it as you can? Instead of that, he has been beside you every moment of your life from your very cradle. It was he who put into your heart those wishes you speak of about being a better man : how else did they ever come there ? You failed, because you did not recognize the hand that led you, and grasp it tight. He has hurt and humbled you in your friend's disgrace, with a plainer view of your own sinfulness and ill desert. By that very thing, you might know he is at your right hand now."

Tom was looking at him with an earnest gaze. " You are not a visionary man, Seelye," he said ; "and, as I live, I believe that what you say is true. Tell me, what then ?"

" Why, then," said John, " he loves you, and is waiting to put into you the virtue you have not. And your duty is to expect the gift, to pray to him for it, to keep turning to him in thought and supplication, from moment to moment, and from hour to hour, in dread lest you should neglect to receive what he holds out to you. If you will do that, I tell you the truth when I tell you, you will find in yourself not an occasional weak wish, but a constant will and an increasing strength to flee from worldly and debasing pleasures, and to follow after righteousness and godliness. You can never do it alone; but, since you are so dissatisfied with yourself, just try this plan; just believe what I say."

There had always been something child-like about Tom, — confiding, generous, impulsive traits, the best and most attractive part of his disposition. By the grace of God, he was willing now, in his discouragement, to receive with child-like humility and trust this offered hope.

"I do believe you," he said stoutly, his rough face brightening with earnest hope; "I do believe the God that made me can help me. If I got my life from him, it must be as you say, that he will give me virtue enough with it to make it worth having. Only — only " — (O Cyril, hear what is his stumbling-block!) " did not Rivers believe in him? He said he did, you know. He kept the Sabbath, and went to the communion. Why was he left, then?"

"Is he left?" asked John. "Why he has

been especially dealt with, and the reason why he got so far away, was because he trusted in himself, — the very opposite reason from that by which you go to God. I tell you, neither Sabbaths nor Sunday schools, nor yet the sacrament, can save a man who by them all is not trying to keep near to God, to receive his grace, and be kept in obedience to his will. The man who lives in self-seeking and self-trust need not expect all the ordinances and means of grace to keep him safe. His eyes must be opened to see his need, and to see his Saviour, before he can be helped ; and it seems to me that is what God means to do for Rivers by all this humiliation and sorrow. But, then, Raddon, don't think of those who profess obedience and do not act it. There are good people enough to prove God's grace, people far too good for any natural disposition to have made them so. Just look about you and think of them. Oh, I wish I could tell you how happy it makes me to see them ! They are a living assurance of the promises. ' I will put my laws in their hearts,' God says ; ' *I will write them upon their minds.*'

' We will come unto him, and make our abode with him.' ' Him that overcometh will I make a pillar in the temple of my God, and he shall go no more out, and I will write upon him the name of my God.' And again: '*He can not sin, because he is born of God.*' Oh, what promises! and to see people that are living witnesses of their truth! I thank God for the sight every day ; but I can never thank him enough."

John's face shone as he spoke. He was now confiding to Tom the loftiest and strongest hopes of his life, and all the joy he felt in the certainty of their achievement.

Those good people he had in mind were some, no doubt, who were raised far above him by age and position, — men such as that pure-minded and pious scholar, that gentle and cultured Christian, who presided over the university ; or as some of its professors, to whom all sciences were only studies of the thoughts of God, expressed in his works ; men clothed with holiness and humility, knowledge and love. They walked as saints to John's eyes, and he thanked God for his hope in following after.

But Tom, as he answered, sighing, "Yes, there are good people, almost as good as the angels, I believe," had in his mind no bent, wrinkled, gray-beard figure, but the vision of one young and fair, and gayly clad, with face that often gleamed with mirth, but, as he fancied it now, looked upon him with bright, startled, indignant eyes, as it had rebuked him when he had once foolishly boasted of sinful conduct.

Ah, well! God has different instruments for different hearts; and a visible beauty and grace must express to some what eyes more enlightened can discern in the spirit under any ancient, worn, and faded garb. But the lightest-hearted maiden that ever won a man to thoughts of a nobler, truer life, is none the less God's instrument than the grave teachers whom long years of grace and experience have trained to do his work.

Notwithstanding new resolves, and all John's counsels and encouragements, Tom went away with some fear and trembling still in his heart, lest the new light he seemed to have found should again vanish in darkness, as good thoughts had passed away from his mind before.

As he walked on in this mood, he passed the college bookstore, a room in one of the buildings, where second-hand text-books of every description were for sale. It came into his mind that he would buy a Bible; for he had none. Think of that, dear reader! — in this land, where a Bible is the child's first well-remembered birthday gift, his Sunday-school prize, the parting token of love and tender anxiety his mother puts into his hand when he leaves home, her dying legacy, — in this land where the gift of a Bible is the commonest expression of Christian charity, or the priceless sign of fondest affection. I wonder if there is one of you who has been so friendless that he was suffered to grow to manhood in the need of purchasing for himself the book of God! But poor Tom had no Bible. If he had had a mother, even the most irreligious, I can not think it would have been so. But his father had almost forgotten that such a book existed : it was the last thing he would have thought of as a necessary item of his boy's outfit when he sent him from home ; and Tom, obliged to have one in school, had left it behind him when he came to college, and never discovered his poverty without it till this minute.

He went into the bookstore and asked for one. The request seemed to surprise the student who waited there. It was such an unusual one, he was not sure he could comply with it. He climbed upon a stool, and hunted among the books upon the high shelves, and in the back corners, until at last he brought forth a much-abused volume, bound in faded red morocco, with broken clasps. Its strong binding held it all together; but idle hands, inconceivably wanton, had cut and defaced the cover, so that it was very shabby. It might have been, nevertheless, a mother's or a sister's gift, which some foolish boy had cast away with other books, less precious, and profited by as little as this. Tom cared little about its looks : it was a Bible, — that was the chief thing to

22

him at present. He paid for it at once, and hastened away.

Seated in his room, he opened the book, to meet, where his eyes first fell upon the page, such words as these : —

"I stretch forth my hands unto thee : my soul thirsteth after thee as a thirsty land."

He paused, his whole heart shaken by the importunate cry with which it echoed those words. But that cry was expressed with yet more craving in the next verse.

"Hear me speedily, O Lord! my spirit faileth : hide not thy face from me, lest I be like to them that go down into the pit."

Yes, this was the true voice of the longing and the fear he had brought from John Seelye's; and from out of it, as did the song, so did Tom's soul rise to trembling trust.

"Cause me to hear thy loving-kindness in the morning ; for in thee do I trust : cause me to know the way in which I should walk ; for I lift up my soul unto thee.

"Deliver me, O Lord, from mine enemies : I flee unto thee to hide me."

It was the refuge that John had showed, that Tom had accepted. He was praying the words that he read with passionate earnestness.

" Teach me to do thy will, for thou art my God; thy spirit is good; lead me into the land of uprightness.

" Quicken me, O Lord, for thy name's sake ; for thy righteousness' sake bring my soul out of trouble."

Do you not think the God of his life answered that prayer ? Indeed it was so. The God who had made and watched over him, at this hour took him by the hand to lead him out of evil habits, out of ignorance, out of a nature full of depravity, through many falls and conflicts, into the land of uprightness.

I have something more to say of Tom ; but I can not say it here. I must go back now to the main personage of my story.

CHAPTER XVIII.

THE LESSON LEARNED.

"Our Lord Jesus Christ, by whom we have now received the
atonement."

WE left Cyril in a bitter hour, or-
phaned and disgraced.   He was at
first bewildered by the suddenness
of the blows that had fallen upon
him; but when the morning dawned,
by the light of the bright spring sunshine, by
the sound of the voices and footsteps of busy
people in the streets, by the knowledge that
penetrated into the hushed and darkened house
of the world outside, awakened again to its
every-day work and hopes and pleasures, the
force of contrast made real to Cyril his
changed position.   The truth of all that had
happened became clear to him ; and his situation, in consequence, was made plain.   Friends

and acquaintances were removed from him by the knowledge of his deed whispered from one to another. Admiration was turned into contempt, favor into indignation. Classmates must be ashamed of his name,—a name whose disgrace was irretrievable, the name of one called a gentleman, and convicted of dishonor; of one professedly a Christian, yet found guilty of deliberate and audacious deceit. Oh, what shame and bitterness were in his soul, as by the morning light he saw these things!

But there was a still greater distress for him in the remembrance of his relations to his mother and sisters. They were weeping in sore grief over their beloved; and in addition, even in these first hours of mourning, prospective poverty and loss of home intruded their terrifying faces. But Cyril knew of a blow to fall upon those burdened hearts, in comparison with which present sufferings would seem light; and it was to come through him, the very one chiefly looked to for strength and solace. Judge whether he was yet so hardened in selfishness that he could look forward to this, and not feel his heart sink in misery, enduring a punishment that seemed to him greater than he could bear.

Whichever way he turned, there was darkness in the future. He had cut himself off from hope. Opportunity had gone with friends and reputation. The church must discard him with the college. Where could he even earn bread for himself and those dependent upon him, when the story of his disgrace had gone abroad, and branded him as a forger and deceiver?

Bowed down that day in such wretchedness as he could not have conceived of before, there was no friend from whom he could ask the relief of sympathy. His mother did not know all; no one else here knew. Ah, if his father could have lived a little longer! if Cyril could have called him back far enough from the mists of death to make him understand all! Cyril had longed to make him comprehend in that dying hour; -but, if he had succeeded, he thought his father would not have listened so peacefully, so calmly; would have had more words to say than those few, " There is the atonement, my son!" as if in those he had said all that was needful, all that human love and wisdom could say.

But, however the case might be, those words were all that Cyril had of hope or help in his trouble ; and his mind clung to them in its desperation, as to a rope from which confused seas of misery tried to beat him away, — a rope that hung slack under his grasp, that fell from out of clouds and darkness, and that he could not yet find any hope to make him believe could draw him to the shore of safety. Yet it was all he had to lay hold of ; and he clung to it, though it seemed to go down with him under the waves.

" The atonement!" Cyril had heard of it from very childhood. Once he fancied that he understood its import ; but now the words seemed unmeaning. Another had suffered for his sins ; that would save him everlasting punishment, it was said, if he would put trust in the deed. But would it save his mother the anguish and shame, his sisters the bitter weeping, his sins were going to give them? Would it save the shadow thrown upon his father's memory, because of having brought up such a son? Would it save to himself the opportunities lost, the blighted life, the friends and pleasures gone? Would it save to his classmates the shaken faith in truth and manhood, and in the power of the Christianity he professed? Would it save his scholars in the Sunday school the awful lesson that all he had taught in the name of truth was but a winning tale, yet idle and meaningless, justly scoffed at by the profane as a fabric of hypocrisy and folly? Would it save the Church of Christ the reproach it must suffer from the open sin of one brought up in its bosom, and enrolled among its members? How could that be called an atonement for his sins which did not save the hurt they had done?

These thoughts wearied and baffled him when he would find comfort. Yet again and again, in the midst of his confusion and perplexity, the words, "But there is the atonement, my son," and the assured and satisfied tone in which they were spoken, would sound in his ears, as if some instinct in his soul, or, perhaps, the unrecognized Comforter there, knew that their simple repetition had enough in it to refute all that the whispers of the Tempter could suggest. And so Cyril could not but revolve those words in his thoughts, till, what with desperate longing, and what with remembrances of good and faithful teaching, and what with being beaten down to the ground in humiliation, he found his way to some knowledge of their truth.

Will you bear with me while I detail some of the workings of his mind upon this subject? They may unfold to us, as to him, something good and precious to remember.

He found a clew that led him some steps toward the light, in this thought first of all: this church that he had injured — it was not merely a collection of men agreed upon certain beliefs, theories beneficial to mankind, that they were anxious to propagate; it was, instead, the cause of God upon earth. In offending against the church, then, it was God against whom he had offended, — God, its founder and its life. Those Sunday-school children — they were not merely individuals whom Cyril had thrown back toward ignorance and sin, the causes of their suffering: they were God's children, it was their Father who was wounded by their hurt. The widow and the fatherless, too, were his special care, and it was God who was grieved in the increase of their grief. And when Cyril had maltreated himself, wasted his time and talents, injured his soul, and thrown away his good name, it was against his Maker and Master still that he had sinned. All other pleas, his own and the world's, were swallowed up in this one, God's. Every other accuser, angry or sorrowful, faded away into the background, and left to Cyril's perception only the vision of this great One, God. It filled his mind: there was no room in his imagination for any thing else. There seemed no room in the world. Upon his right hand and his left hand, before him and behind him, was God; he was surrounded by God. What could he do, overtaken by this conviction, but to cry out, " Against Thee, and *Thee only*, have I sinned, and done this evil in thy sight!"

Yes, in God's sight! There was no other eye to be taken account of by Cyril now. How strange that he had once chiefly dreaded that parents and friends should know his deed, when all along he had been in God's sight! The thought of that one gaze overwhelmed him now: whither could he flee from it? where hide himself from its penetration?

Oh! he remembered now how the stranger who had found him out had spoken of an hour when he might call to the rocks to fall upon him and hide him. This was not the hour, though he was so conscious, in his sinfulness, of God's sight; why not? why not?

His groping mind caught another clew. Why? because there was the atonement, the atonement still available! Against God he had sinned, and to God had the atonement been made. That it must be sufficient, the instinctive spring with which his heart leaped to seize the thought was witness enough if he had not his father's testimony and that of the Scriptures. In the joy and relief of this, other hopeful thoughts crowded fast into his mind. God must have meant the name of that sacrifice to have its full meaning, and by it, then, in some way, might Cyril not hope his sins would be nullified, — those heavy sins, that had weighed him down with anguish? He, indeed, could see no way to rectify their consequences to himself or others ; but, since they were atoned for, might he not believe God had found a way ? that there was a good He had set over against the evil that vanquished it ; nay, that could bring goodness out of it, as flowers spring out of a bloody field, — the same good that, as was sung long, long ago, could bring praise out of the wrath of man ?

Cyril had only a glimpse of all that was in this thought at that hour, though he saw enough to comfort him ; but, through many after-years, this view of the atonement served him as a subject to ponder over with unspeakable wonder and thankfulness. He gradually gained a clearer understanding of it. He saw Christ to be far, far more in benefit to his church than the harm of all the sins of men against it. He saw Christ found in despair by transgressors to be sweeter than their hard way down into the depths had been bitter. He saw Christ the Comforter, found in sorrow, more precious than the grief was hard. All his life long he rejoiced to watch the workings of this wonderful alchemy, which brings glory out of shame, strength out of weakness, joy out of sorrow, and which shall prevail more and more upon the earth till the day of atoning is past, because sin has dominion no more.

Cyril had need of all the spiritual comfort and strength he could obtain, in the bitter trials, that, after that first day, came thick and fast upon him. His father had not been laid in the grave before the altered looks toward himself of the people who came to the house showed that his story had reached his native town. And at last one of his father's deacons came for a private interview with him. He had a painful duty to undertake, he said, both as

Cyril's brother church-member, and as one
who loved him for his father's sake. He had
brought both stories that had been published in
Eaton, and he must hear the truth of them
from Cyril's own lips. Cyril told it as well as
he could for agitation and shame. He pleaded
no apology, and asked no leniency : that would
have seemed bold, in view of the enormity of
what he had done. He did not urge his peni-
tence : that was too cheap and easy a thing to
weigh against his sin. He told the simple
story, submitting to the result. That story,
and the sight of the culprit, moved the old
man, between wonder, indignation, and grief,
to great excitement, which must find expression. He did not understand Cyril's not making any effort at self-extenuation, and the quietness of his utter humiliation. He could not
help admonishing the young man whom God
had already so effectually warned; he must
remind him how the blow would fall upon his
mother : as if no agony had already been suffered at that thought! he must point out again
all the sad consequences : as if they had been

out of the sinner's mind one moment through the last two days!

He was a good and kind man; but such a flagrant offense as this had never come within the sphere of his action before, and he knew not how to treat it. It appeared to him that Cyril never could be reproved enough. He was the only worldly dependence of his mother and sisters; and such a revelation of the worthlessness of his character at this time was terrible. No wonder the old man was exceedingly agitated and distressed! He talked long to poor Cyril of the guilt and disgrace he had incurred, without perceiving how forcibly it had already been impressed upon him, or without suggesting to him any possibility of his ever being able to retrieve the wrongs he had committed.

But Cyril saw now, that, whatever compassion might be felt in the parish toward his mother, the story could not long be kept from her. And though he knew the suffering it must cause her, yet he longed to have her know it, longed for her forgiveness and counsel. It only remained to choose the time to tell her. It seemed to him, that, should he wait till after his father's funeral, in the dreary time of the first utter loneliness in the house, and when preparations for removal, and plans for the sad future, must be undertaken, the blow would fall more heavily than now. Beside his father's coffin, where the peaceful face would seem to repeat to them both the comfort that had satisfied the good man in death, only there Cyril felt that he could tell his mother. And there he did tell her, turning ever and anon toward that still face for help to bear the sight of the pain, the grief, the agitation he read upon hers, as he traced the story from the commencement of his college course down to the last shameful details. She could not hide from him the dismay and sorrow with which they overwhelmed her, though she had thought her heart dulled by the first grief to all events that could follow. But she had drawn near to God, and was keeping there for help to bear her loss, and so was ready to reach out her hand for his support in this new affliction.

And, moreover, she saw how great the peril of Cyril's soul had been, and that God had been dealing with him by his providences and his grace, so as to make him thoroughly humble and repentant. She would have been no true mother, if, in the midst of disappointed pride and trust, she yet could not feel some thankfulness for his correction.

So she had no reproaches for him, only forgiveness and sympathy and counsel. If it had not been, afterward, for a new confidence placed by her in him, and for her love and help when all the world distrusted him, and met him with coldness and rebuff, I know not how he could have borne the troubles of those shaded years of his entrance upon active life.

A day or two after his father's funeral, Cyril received two letters from Eaton. One, in Tom Raddon's peculiar handwriting and orthography, written very earnestly and affectionately, told the story of the writer's actions and emotions since he parted from Cyril, and in what new beliefs he had found comfort. It was full of sympathy, and full of repentance; and it touched Cyril not only by the unshaken love it revealed, and by the simply-told story of all Tom had done for him, but by the manner in which it seemed to take for granted in him a right state of feeling under all these troubles. Tom showed no more fear and distrust for him than if he had never known him do wrong. For this, and for all Tom's generosity, it seemed to Cyril that he never could be grateful enough. Very humbling thoughts came with the feeling. He looked back to the hour when Tom had first seized his half-unwilling hand, and vowed to be his friend, and saw, that, all the way from that time to this, the one he had secretly looked down upon had played the noble part in their companionship. Upon Tom's side, friendship had been no false seeming, put on for convenience, or worn from indolence and good-nature. He had been always faithful to the extent of his knowledge, and had signally proved the genuineness of his affection in these dark hours at the last.

The other letter was from the college faculty, dismissing Cyril from his connection with the institution. He had expected that. He could not, under any circumstances, have returned to college ; but the little note might well revive a long train of sorrowful reflections. It had ended in this, then, — that college career that was begun with so many hopes ! The years that were to have furnished him with power to attain a high place in life had left him despoiled of reputation, well-nigh crushed with disgrace. The time and the place that were to have witnessed the beginning of honors won had known his name conspicuous only for shame.

But even while poor Cyril, with heavy heart, and eyes dimmed with sorrowful tears, gazed upon that note, there came to him a faint whisper of comfort and peace. "Nevertheless," said this voice, "it is not all lost. Since you have turned to Him, God is so merciful, he will redeem something for you out of what you have so recklessly flung away. Here is a lesson he teaches you out of your college course, that is better than all other learning without it : he whom the Lord upholds alone is safe ; he who has set the Lord *always* before him, whose eyes are *ever* toward the Lord, whose cry is unto him evening and morning and at noon, — he only shall surely not be moved : the God whose atonement can deliver thy soul from death is the only Power whose wisdom can keep thy feet from falling. God has brewed a bitter drink for you out of the fruits of your folly ; but through his goodness it is a wine of strength. The jewel you lightly esteemed at first he has forced you at last to stoop low, and painfully to find : but it is humility and the fear of the Lord ; its gain makes light the loss of laurels and renown. He is so true and gracious, that he has done better for you than you would ask. He will make up all the wanton waste if you will be his disciple, and henceforth seek to follow him as faithfully, as watchfully, as he has followed you. There is this still left for you, — to thank him with your life."

But Cyril's lesson was learned at a great cost ; it was forced upon his heedless heart only after severe and terrible punishment. May it not answer in place of such sad personal experience, — experience whose teaching, alas ! is sometimes read all too late, — to others as careless and as confident as he? Of all who were shocked at his fall, there were few of his companions to trace its causes back to the slight deceptions, the trifling indulgences in vanity, of which others were as guilty as he. Yet nothing is surer than the connection. If it had not been for his familiarity with sin, he would not have risked so boldly, and lost his honor. Friends, we can none of us prophesy of ourselves, or tell how far we shall be carried, when we say, that, in little things, it matters not whether we take the easy instead of the upright way. When we are accustomed to such reasoning, the sin to which there is any temptation will always seem a little thing. Let us rather ask God to fix in us the conviction that no transgression is small. Then we shall be first cleansed from secret faults, and so for ever kept back from presumptuous sins.

What I might have put in a preface, — a few words about one of my reasons for writing this story, — it seems to me will be better understood here. It was partly suggested to me by hearing some young persons talking lightly of practices such as purchasing essays from a ready writer, to read in the class, and the like, although events very similar to those narrated in the latter part of this story had but recently shocked them, as well as the rest of the community. Not only had their careless eyes seen no connection between the little deceits and the great ones, but so blunted had their moral sense become by the prevalence of bad habits, that in the former they scarcely seemed to see any sin at all. But these cheating tricks of boyish cunning that are so commonly practiced in every school and college throughout the land; that the best-principled youth scarcely lift their voices to condemn; that parents and guardians often wink at, or perhaps openly laugh about and applaud; and that teachers vainly and half-despairingly strive to weed out, —are not of little account. The notions so recklessly adopted at school are carried from thence into business and political life. The youth who cheats for the benefit of his class or his division will cheat for his firm or his party soon. The youth who begs or buys the services of his classmate to help him to a station he has not earned, will, before long, buy the services of the forger and the counterfeiter, to make him a millionnaire, or will buy lying orators and unprincipled voters to make him a governor or a senator. And after the most flagrant wickedness, the most utter meanness, he and his coadjutors, called by the world respectable men, defended with virtuous indignation from all attacks by their party organs, will laugh together in their conclaves over the smart wire-pulling, the cunning tricks, with the same unconcern with which the schoolboys among themselves boasted of the deception of their tutor as a good joke. And all the while our country's trade and government languish in every part, from fraud and corruption, the unscrupulous selfishness of private citizens everywhere making rotten the foundations upon which rests the welfare of the community.

The warning is not the remedy; but there is a remedy, and I point it out — listen, young people and children — not to your teachers and parents, but to you. I have that faith in your love of your country, and in your anxiety to be a benefit to it, that I believe you will strive after the safeguard yourselves. It is in the fear of the Lord, which is clean, and in the commandment of the Lord, which is pure. There is One who desireth truth in the inward parts, and who is of purer eyes than to behold iniquity. Ask him to be continually with you, to hold you by the right hand, to guide you with his counsel, to create in you a clean heart, and to renew a right spirit within you. Ask him not to cast you away from his presence; not to take his Holy Spirit from you for an hour, for a moment. And he will be gracious to you, teach you his ways, and make you *delight* to do his will. I can not continue Cyril's history much farther, to show how what he learned from his college course was still more deeply impressed upon his mind by the trials of the following years, by all the humiliations and difficulties arising from his disgrace that beset him in the struggle to obtain a livelihood. His mother moved to the nearest large town, to support herself by taking boarders; and his sisters, by hard endeavor, found opportunity to earn the scanty pay of teachers; but, wherever Cyril tried to obtain even the humblest employment, the old story would waken prejudice against him. To win back trust and his good name, to get even the least opportunity to do it, for a long time seemed well-nigh impossible. Not only must he suffer in this himself, but he must see his family suffer also. He learned to be very meek and patient, very unselfish and thoughtful, while his trust in God kept him from being utterly cowed and discouraged, and a sense of his desert withheld him from repining. The powers of his mind were developed and matured by his combat with adversity. He had an object in winning the victory, — to make some recompense to the dear friends he had so injured; and he was successful at last. He outlived the story of his disgrace, and gained respect and influence. But all the days of his life he walked softly, carrying a memory that admonished him, and that kept his heart fixed in God's fear.

I know my story is properly finished here ; but I am going to add, as a sort of sequel to it, a chapter about Tom, because the story of his after-course seems to me so interesting.   But I can only sketch it very briefly.

CHAPTER XIX.

A LITTLE MORE ABOUT TOM.

" It is God that guideth me with strength, and maketh my way perfect."

WHAT Tom had begun he had begun in earnest. His heart was set steadfastly toward a new life. As frank and unashamed as he had been in his ignorance and heathenism, so was he in his new knowledge and entrance upon Christianity. He freely told his companions what new thoughts and beliefs he had ; and they watched him with astonishment, yielding himself up with childlike docility to his persuasions. Most of them considered him under the effect of an excitement that would soon pass away. But the victories he gained over himself, the new manliness developed in him by the workings of that Spirit to which he had surrendered himself, were an undeniable reality. His mind seemed almost suddenly to have developed and matured. In the hope of usefulness, he began to judge concerning his own welfare as no selfish wisdom could have taught him to do.

One of his first acts was to go to Professor M'Tafor, and confess how he had gained that prize a whole year since, restoring the money, and asking that the story might be made as public as Cyril's disgrace had been. For the sake of justice, this was reluctantly done in his class, and among the competitors whom he had cheated. But it was the case, as he had once angrily declared it would be, that his genuine repentance and his confession saved him from reproach, and won him the free forgiveness of teachers and classmates. Indeed, the kind feeling toward him among the latter had pardoned his half-suspected offense long ago.

It was a more daring matter to make the same confession to his father, and to tell of many other deceits and bad habits, of his conviction that he was incompetent to go on with his class, and his desire to be allowed to go back to the one below. The honest, sorrowful letter in which all this was told, Tom, as he sent it away, verily believed would withdraw him from college at once, and set him at work among Chinamen and sailors, to oversee the lading and unlading of his father's ships under the burning suns upon San-Francisco Bay.

But his father was a shrewd man, and, in the midst of anger and disappointment, he discovered at last the ring of manly earnestness and sincerity in Tom's strange letter. And Tom was his only son, and he could not yet quite give up his long-cherished ambition with regard to him. He cut down Tom's allowance, for punishment, and sent him some angry threats, but bade him, notwithstanding, go into the class below, as he desired, and begin again.

Tom set himself to the task with patience and diligence. He had to struggle hard with old habits and depraved tastes ; but the struggle was not so long nor so doubtful as might have been supposed. New affections springing up cast the old into the shade, and, by degrees, withered their baneful life. The main features of Tom's conversion were his sudden discovery of God's reality and nearness, and his hope and joyful confidence in that knowledge. His heavenly Father was not far from him at any time, and was able to bestow strength. Tom must hourly press closer to him to receive it. There was once one, who, in his first humble prayer, was answered, " *To-day* shalt thou be with me in paradise." That man, indeed, was then almost beyond the dominion of the prince of this world, beyond the reach of temptation ; yet the change that made him ready for paradise, his soul's reception of righteousness from Christ, must have been an instantaneous change. And when we have counted all our hinderances, from foes within and foes without, is there, then, sufficient reason to excuse our slow, hardly apparent growth in grace ? Is not the true cause found in our lingering unwillingness to suffer the change to be put upon us ? We hang back from self-surrender, and think of our own watchfulness and self-government as our hope of holiness. We would be

always remembering ourselves, instead of saying, " Lord, remember me !" We think of
keeping our hearts with all diligence, and forget that the diligence is vain which aims only
to keep them swept and garnished, and not to
have them full of Christ. To be with him in
paradise is to be perfectly safe ; and upon earth
to be much in communion with him, the fore-
taste of paradise, is our only security. If we
had a more continual consciousness of his
presence and help, we should not find the
advantage over sin so hardly and slowly won.
Such a consciousness was given to Tom ; and,
while he rejoiced in it, it was wonderful how
he was changed.

In the course of the two following years,
from the saddest of all sights, an indolent,
unreasoning, impulse-governed man, he became thoughtful, patient, and unselfish, with
powers developed and under command, and
activities that were awake, and in earnest to
improve himself and the world ; and, at the end
of those two years, he had grown so refined in
manners, so brightened and improved in looks,

and was so respected in reputation, that there was no one of Mary Owens' friends to wonder or regret when she promised him her hand.

Tom overcame his idle habits and natural inaptitude for study, so as to graduate with a very good appointment. And at that time his father made the journey all the way from San Francisco, to see his son for the first time upon a public stage. The old man looked about upon the new world of men and things in this Eastern city, wise enough to acknowledge an advanced civilization in it for all its plainness and quietness, its want of wealth and commerce and crowds; and no words could express the satisfaction and triumph with which he compared his son with the cultivated men among whom he found him, and perceived him able to sustain the comparison. The success was beyond all he had hoped. His Tom had not become the pretentious, loud-voiced, unprincipled demagogue that had been once the father's idea of a politician, but something that he could understand was better and more effective, in proportion as it was rarer in public life : a man soundly instructed, firmly principled, with an enlightened will and an independent judgment, — "A man that can go alone!" said Mr. Raddon to himself with delight, — "a man that don't need to be boosted, and can't be tricked !"

But he never imagined how all this had come about. He supposed it the result of his own liberality and shrewdness in sending Tom to college, together with the youth's natural cleverness and goodness. He would have been utterly astonished and unbelieving if it had been told him that One had done more for his child, out of love and infinite charity, than all the teachers and the books that money could provide ; and that, but for the intervention of that One, Tom would in all probability have come away from college to be only a shame and disappointment, perhaps a drunkard, or an indolent, vice-crippled wreck of manhood, in whom neither threats nor promises could have awakened again the feeblest impulse of energy or ambition. So the old man went about boasting, thanking his gods, — his money and himself, — and never thought of the Giver of all, who was so patient with his ignorance.

Nevertheless, there was something very touching in the father's perfect pleasure, as he sat in the commencement-hall, and listened to Tom's speech. When it was through, and Tom was speeded off the stage with the customary round of applause from his friends, the old man looked about, his face radiant with pride and satisfaction, and actually bowed his thanks to the people around him, as if the tribute had been bestowed upon himself. He was as proud of Tom's engagement, too, as of his other achievements. Even old Ruel Raddon could believe that this young lady was one not to be bought with money: so that Tom's winning her — such a genuine lady, educated, refined, and pretty enough to be an earl's daughter — was in itself another proof of his superiority.

You will understand that his father's visit must have been a little trying to Tom in the first flush of his triumph in his engagement and his graduation. It can not be denied that the old man's red face, the gaudy dress he had provided himself, the ungrammatical and boastful style of his conversation, and his constant recourse to ardent spirits for stimulus, disturbed Tom in presenting his father among new friends of such a different style. But Tom was too warm-hearted and honest to let any such false shame trouble him much; and his feelings of annoyance were soon forgotten in serious regret, because his father was so far from him in the things that made the light and fullness of his life. Tom began to see the work that lay before him more plainly now. He had resolved to study law, and begin practicing in his native place in accordance with the old plan. But how differently now he looked upon that plan! It was no more to his view an idler's scheme for cheating and bribing his way into office, pandering to corrupt party interests: it was to be an honest man's path of industrious service to God and his generation. In a city full of men like his father, and worse, he was to advocate truth and right, in spite of all inducements to knavery; publicly and privately, he was to stand up for principle in the fear of God, and to promote, with all his influence, the causes of justice and purity and religion.

It was not till he had fairly entered upon his work, that his father found out all the diversity of intentions between them. The old man's first idea was to push Tom into public favor by every means, fair and foul. To his dismay, he found an insuperable obstacle to such proceedings in Tom himself. A man who would not say what he did not believe; who would not slander either a party or an individual for his own advancement; a man who would not advocate a wrong measure, however popular; a man who fought the dearest vices of the community, with law or without law, stirring up by his merciful endeavors the wrath and hatred of all its profligates; a man who would be always remembering the very pariahs of the city, vexing himself for their wrongs, degrading himself with openly-expressed concern for despised foreigners, their ignorance and abuse, — judge of old Ruel Raddon's dismay, when he began to find such a man in his own son!

He had long known of Tom's religion, and had acquiesced in it as something, that, in some indefinite way, as Greek or Latin or poetry had done, had tended to make him a gentleman, — something that was a part of the intelligence and refinement that made him superior. As a thing of that description, he had no objection to it ; but when he discovered it to be something that led the young man to sacrifice profit to principle, when he saw Tom, for its sake, running counter to current opinion, exciting hostile remark, growing decidedly unpopular, the old man began to be very angry. He tried in vain persuasions and remonstrances, threats and sneers. The young man was sorely tried ; but he persisted in his course. For months at a time, his father's anger would be so hot against him, that he could not speak peaceably to him, and often he would not speak to him at all. But these quarrels were kept close between them. It was a curious thing that the father's jealousy for his son's welfare was yet so strong, that, while he reproached him at home, he upheld him abroad, always defended him with shrewdness and vehemence.

It was years before the difference, so trying to the souls of both, was ended. But at last old Mr. Raddon, finding opposition useless, began in his secret soul to acknowledge the beauty and the goodness of his son's course. His thoughts toward him grew lenient. By degrees, Tom's opinions were tolerated, then approved, at last adopted with unbounded admiration. Moreover, the old man found himself not alone in this change. Tom had made progress in winning the hearts and enlightening the consciences of other men, by his integrity, his earnestness, and his benevolence. He had *made* the party and the public opinion to sustain him. His father lived to see him an honored and successful man, and, leaning upon his son in perfect trust as he went down toward the dark valley of the shadow of death, was willing at last to receive the faith that had been to Tom salvation.

Thus I have briefly sketched Tom's career, to show how it was affected by what befell him in college. Ah! if there were more as fortunate as he in the years of seedtime. But I will not write that sigh despondingly; for the free grace and loving-kindness of God are ever abundant, and his providence is favorable to every soul. And then the Church of God, I know, has always that cause of thankfulness for you, young people, with which St. Paul rejoiced over Timothy: "*I thank God, that, without ceasing, I have remembrance of thee in my prayers night and day.*"